Moons Tale

By Lindsay Uvery

Copyright © 2014 by Lindsay Uvery
First Edition – April 2014

ISBN
978-1-4602-1067-3 (Hardcover)
978-1-4602-1065-9 (Paperback)
978-1-4602-1066-6 (eBook)

All rights reserved.

No part of this publication may be reproduced in any form, or by any means, electronic or mechanical, including photocopying, recording, or any information browsing, storage, or retrieval system, without permission in writing from the publisher.

Produced by:

FriesenPress
Suite 300 – 852 Fort Street
Victoria, BC, Canada V8W 1H8

www.friesenpress.com

Distributed to the trade by The Ingram Book Company

My name is Liz, I am 24 years old and I live in a small city named Prince Albert, Saskatchewan. The house I live in is small and on the east side of the city. I am a student whose main focus is business.

I am a petite girl with long brown hair with blonde highlights. If you look closely you'll see my eyes are blue. Although Prince Albert can be boring at times I always find ways to have fun. Although my social life is limited because I have so little time, I do try and go out with my friends for coffee and drinks. I thought my life seemed pretty normal, that is until I learned something that turned my world upside down. Strange things began to happen, I started to change, but I don't mean change as in I grew or that I changed my hair colour. This change was weird.

Chapter One

The Beginning

As I lay there awake, wishing I could fall asleep only for a little bit longer, my mind was racing with thoughts. I looked towards the clock, today was Saturday. I could sleep in.
  "It's only 6:00 in the morning I would really like to have slept in." I told myself as I pulled the covers over my head, determined to rest some more.
  I eventually worked up enough energy to get out of bed, put my hair in a ponytail and get dressed. I heard howling, whatever it was it sounded as if it was right in front of my house. I opened the window and looked outside in the early morning light, and nothing, but I could still hear the howling. I stuck my head out the window and foolishly howled back. To my surprise whatever or whoever was doing the howling was returned with another howl so I quickly closed the window tight shut. As I was going down the stairs to get ready for my morning jog I caught a glimpse of something in the corner of my eye, I ran down the stairs in fear. I quickly turned on the kitchen light looked around, but of course, there was nothing there. I shook my head and laughed to myself, as I grabbed a bottle of water. I headed to the front door, ready for my morning jog and just as I was about to open it I felt something pass quickly behind me, it was cold and it made the hairs on the back of my neck stand up. I could feel goose bumps forming under my sweater. I stood motionless, trying to figure out what it was that made me feel so frightened. I finally told myself

Liz you're going crazy it's nothing. Just calm down and breathe. So I did. I took a deep breath and headed out the door. I jog for about an hour each day, always in the morning to get me going for the day. I was heading back to my place when I noticed an unusual dog standing at my door, it looked like a black German shepherd, it appeared angry, as if it was about to attack me at any moment.

"It's a nice puppy, it's okay, I won't hurt you," I said hoping this might calm the dog down. But no such luck. Oh great, now what am I going to do? I can't even get back into my own house. "What a great way to start my day off." I muttered to myself as I tried not to stare the dog in the eyes.

"Zeus! Come here, Zeus. Leave that poor lady alone!" It was man's voice calling from a distance. He rushed toward me. "I am so sorry. I don't know why he is acting like this. He never does anything like this. He is usually a good dog," the man said. When he was talking I noticed fear in his eyes were darting about nervously

"Don't worry, I get it a lot," I said calmly lying through my teeth, but I didn't want him to feel bad he looks like he has been having a bad day already

"My name is Tyler I live just down the street from here, and I apologize again I don't know what brought that on." Tyler was now holding his dog back, and I could still see the fear in his eyes.

Tyler was super cute, I figured he was about 5'9" tall and about 200 pounds, you could tell he was well built the way he was holding Zeus back I could feel his baby blue eyes ran up and down my body as he ran his fingers through his dirty blonde hair .You could tell he was getting annoyed at the curls.

He said in a British accent, "No matter how short I cut it, it still gets annoying. I'm not too sure how long I want to keep this goatee either it's getting kind of unmanageable."

I chuckled at him and smiled. I then spoke up before things got more awkward then they already were. "Nice to meet you Tyler, my name is Liz and this is my house, and again it's okay really so don't worry about it." I lied. Deep down I was scared shitless because of the uncontrollable dog.

I looked at Zeus, and he looked back at me. Then he started whining and trying to escape Tyler's grip on his lead. I couldn't understand why this dog had decided to hate me so much. What was it about me that frightened this dog so much? I was so confused. I have never had this happen to me before. What was going on with me? That is all I could keep thinking, I knew I had to talk to someone about this but the question was who? Who would I talk to about these strange and recent occurrences? Yeah, they would probably lock me away and pump me full of anti-psychotics. I just stared into space and realised that I now couldn't move.

"Liz, Liz? Are you okay?" Tyler asked as he waved his hand in front of my face to see if I would wake up from my zoning.

"Umm, yeah I am okay," I said, quickly shaking my head, embarrassed. I started to walk towards my door, slowly. "Anyways it was nice meeting you and thanks for your help," I said walking up to my door still shaking and wondering.

"Yeah it was nice meeting you too. Kind of a strange way to meet someone, but yeah, you're welcome," Tyler said and waved his hand at me as he laughed to himself. "Come on, Zeus. I don't know what your problem is but I won't put up with that." he told his dog as they walked down the street, back to where they lived.

I realized I could hear every word he was saying no matter how far away he was. And it's not like he was talking loud. I found that very unusual. So what more can go wrong today? I asked myself as I opened my fridge door to pour myself a glass of milk which I gulped right down.

I headed back upstairs and jumped into a nice warm shower. I was feeling relaxed once more when I heard a crash downstairs. I turned off the shower, grabbed a towel, and ran downstairs. Where did that noise come from? It sounded like breaking glass so I scanned the room to see what I had that was breakable that would sound like that. I couldn't think of anything. Finally it hit me. I ran to my spare room and, sure enough, that was what had made the noise an ancient wolf statue it was a medium sized wolf sitting down, the statue was in a howling position it was white in color given by my mom before she passed away. I was in tears trying to find all the pieces hoping I might somehow piece it together again. I was searching around for all the pieces there was a paw by the bed and the head was by the door picking up then head that is when I came across a scroll. I unravelled it but it was in a language I could not understand the scroll was a baby blue color it was about a page long. Daniel. He will know. I phoned my friend Daniel because he had taken courses all over the world in all sorts of languages. Daniel would know.

"Hey, Daniel! Are you busy?" I asked, crossing my fingers hoping he would be able to come over because I was dying to know what this meant.

"No. Why?" Daniel asked sounding a bit concerned.

"Um, I found something in that old wolf statue my mom gave me years ago. Well the thing somehow smashed to the floor and in all the pieces I found a scroll. I can't understand the language that is written on it. So, I was hoping you could come over and help me." I asked sounding desperate.

"Yeah, I can I will be right there," Daniel replied but I thought he sounded kind of annoyed as if I had interrupted him in something important. But instead of asking I said, "Thank you so much" and hung up the phone. I ran upstairs to get dressed.

I got dressed put my hair in a ponytail I threw on some black sweats and zipped up a pink sweater and waited patiently for Daniel. I was nervous and excited at the same time so I just stared at the clock. It shouldn't take that long to get to my house. Prince Albert isn't that big. Ten minutes had passed but it felt like an hour. I kept staring at the clock and about half a minute later I heard a familiar knock at my door. I went flying down my stairs and swung the door wide open and there stood Daniel.

Daniel 6'2", 145 pound frame stood in the doorway. His short brown hair looked really messy it looked like he just crawled out of bed and came over. I still love how his glasses bring out his baby blue eyes. Daniel and I have been good friends since grade 8, so that would be about 7 years now.

"Hello, Liz. Sorry I am late. I had some running around to do first," Daniel apologized as he walked in and took off his shoes.

"That's alright. Besides, I needed to get ready anyways. Have a seat on the couch. Do you want anything to drink?" I asked as I headed towards the kitchen to pour myself a glass of water.

"No thank you, maybe in a bit." Daniel was about to sit down on the couch, he spotted something over in the corner by my TV. It was a dog collar. "Hey, Liz I never knew you had a pet dog!" He picked up the red collar and started playing with it.

"What gave you that idea I had a pet dog?" I asked from the kitchen, my face full of confusion as I headed back towards Daniel.

"Because I found this dog collar lying there on the rug by your TV any ideas on how it got there?" Daniel asked, looking at the dog tags. "The name on this tag says Zeus".

"This is going to sound weird, but this morning when I went for my usual jog I was about to come home and there was a black German shepherd in my yard. And the strangest thing, he wouldn't let me into my house. He just stood there with his hackles up growling at me. It was only when his owner came and shouted at the dog to leave me alone that he eventually stopped. And that dog's name is Zeus. I don't know how and why his collar is in my house though. I have no idea what is going on." I explained the situation to Daniel as I stared at the collar wondering how Zeus's collar got in my house.

"This is really strange and I don't know what to tell you. Anyways, Liz, we will figure that out later. Where is that scroll you wanted me to look at?" Daniel asked as he put his hand on my leg. "Liz, are you going to be alright?" Daniel asked me with a concern look on his face.

"Umm, yeah I will be fine. I will get that scroll." I replied and headed to the spare room to grab the scroll, still holding the collar. I kept wondering how it had ended up in my place. I felt I was going crazy. "Here you go Daniel." I said handing over the scroll to him.

Daniel unravelled the scroll and noticed right away it was German.. He was reading it and he started to shake and I could see whatever he was reading was making him afraid and was starting to scare me. After he was done reading it he looked at me and held my hand.

"Liz are you ready for what I am about to tell you?" he asked me as he squeezed my hand and looked intently into my eyes.

"Yes," I replied, unsure.

"I don't know how to explain this to you, but let me go at another way. How well did you know your mother?" Daniel asked letting go of my hand.

"I didn't really know her too well, I remember us running away a lot from bad people," I replied and then everything went quiet for a few seconds, before Daniel eventually spoke up.

"Well here it goes. According to this scroll you, Liz, are part of the lycanthrope family." Daniel explained as he stared at the message making sure he read it right. He kept glancing over at me.

I tried not to laugh.

"Lycanthrope, meaning werewolf," Daniel explained, as his voice faltering.

"I know what lycanthrope means," I replied as I burst out laughing, I couldn't help myself.

"Liz, this isn't funny. What it explains is that your family are all lycanthropes passed down from generation to generation. Usually the curse strikes right away but in your case there was a spell that was cast upon you so that when you turned 24 that was when the curse was going to take effect. So according to this scroll on the next full moon you will start to transform. Haven't you noticed anything different about yourself?" He asked as he looked upset and concerned at the same time.

"I am sorry," I said, trying to sound serious. "It's just that you seem to expect me to believe I am a werewolf? Come on Daniel werewolves only exist in horror movies. I think someone put that scroll in that wolf statue as a prank just to scare the next person who looks at it. I mean does it even say who wrote it or where it is from? Probably not so that tells me it is a joke." I ranted on then I stopped and starred at Daniel.

He didn't respond. Then I began to think about it. It kind of makes sense. My intense hearing, smell, and the ability to run fast without ever running out of breath. What about Zeus and the way he growled at me? It sounds so crazy but at this point I have nothing else to explain what is going on with me. I knew this was serious so I tried to explain to Daniel, "Now that you got me thinking, yes, strange things have been happening to me recently. I never talked about them because they freak me out. I can hear and smell everything, my ability to run for ever. This episode this morning with Zeus that was strange to," I replied as I looked intently at Daniel.

"I know it is a lot to face right now, but the next full moon is in a few days and I think you need to get prepared," Daniel replied as he carefully rolled the scroll and put on his shoes. "I will look up some more information and come back later tonight. Until then, get some rest Liz," Daniel hugged me and left.

"Ok, bye." I said as I sighed.

I ran up to my room and laid on my bed crying. Although I had Daniel to help me but I still felt alone I mean I have no family. I didn't have a clue what to expect or what to do. What if I hurt people? What if I kill people? Then I sat up. Okay, Liz, get it together, I told myself. I took a deep breath. I will figure out something.

I got up and went downstairs I headed out the door. But before I took off for a walk I wanted to test something. If I was really a werewolf then I should be able to jump off buildings, run fast, and leap a fare distance. So I began climbing up the side of the house toward the roof.

"Liz are you out of your mind? I asked myself as I went to the edge and looked down I saw my shrubs and the top of my vehicle standing there for a few seconds I took a deep breath and jumped. I screamed the whole way down, but lo and behold I landed on my feet. I stood there in shock. My feet didn't even hurt. Wow this is so cool!. Anyway now was the time to get back to my walk. I find that long walks always help when I am unsure about my feelings. I hadn't gone very far when I could hear foot steps behind me. I got scared and I walked faster. And so did the footsteps. "Oh god what now"? I asked myself and I started to run. I went towards the nearest park and sat on one of the swings. I sat, swinging back and forth. Then I realised that a hand was covering my mouth before I could react I was out cold. When I woke up I saw that I was in the passenger's side of a truck, I looked outside it was pretty dark outside so I knew I have been out for a while the driver was driving pretty fast I had no idea where we were. I felt dizzy, nauseas and somewhat in pain. I turned my head and looked at the driver to see if I might recognize who it was, but no such luck.

"Who are you? What do you want?" I asked, struggling hard to speak.

"I see my love is awake," replied the driver, as he looked at me, grinning.

"You didn't answer my questions," I snarled, glaring at him.

"You will soon find out in good time dear. I can't tell you why I kidnapped you, it will be too hard explain while I am driving, love." He turned left and pulled into a gas station.

I struggled to think what was happening it was so hard to process everything. "Did this person know what I was?" I asked myself as I took a deep breath in. His voice was deep but quiet. There was so much running through my mind, I was getting mentally drained.

"Now don't go anywhere, I can't exactly trust you, but if you try and escape I will only find you again" he said as he got out of his truck. As he was filling up his truck I was trying to look through the window to see if I could recognize him, but the window was so dirty I couldn't make out who he was. I looked around the truck the seats where a navy blue they were worn out almost looks like claw marks. I could smell dog it was overwhelming. I quietly slid towards the other side of the truck and slowly opened the door, when I noticed he was inside paying I ran and ran until I almost couldn't run any more. I had no idea where I was so I headed up the road passing lots of trees and shrubs there was no buildings I was hoping to see if a vehicle would notice me. I tried to see if my phone would get any service, but I had no bars. What is the point of having a phone when I can't use it? I swore at the useless phone in my hand and then heard a vehicle behind me. I turned around to see that it was the truck.

"Oh shit!" I yelled and took off running, not looking back.

The truck then pulled to the side of the road, and stopped. I could hear the door open then close I knew that the person that got out of the vehicle was after me I wasn't taking any chances so I bolted .Considering how dark it was outside I could still see where I was going but my sight looked very unusual like everything was a yellow color and sort of fuzzy. I looked back in the darkness I could still see and hear someone running after me. I didn't stick around to make out any details so I took off running again.

In the distance I heard a voice yelling at me. "You're not going to escape!" He was running after me as well and closing the distance between us.

I didn't know who he was or what he wanted with me and I wasn't about to find out without putting up a fight. I ran a little further until I heard or saw nothing behind me anymore so I slowed down to catch my breath and when I thought it might be safe I looked back to see if he was still there. Nothing, so I took a deep breathe in. I started to cry maybe I should just have just stayed with him at least I would have been in a warm truck. Let's face it the weather was nasty the wind was unreal and there was this nasty cold breeze along with the wind. Then I heard a vehicle again and I could see that it was that same truck again. I rolled my eyes and stood still, trying to think what this asshole wants with me. I had no idea where I was going so I just gave up. The driver got out of the truck and grabbed me by the arm and threw me in the passenger's side.

"Ouch! Do you have to be so rough?" I yelled, rubbing my arm.

"Well, love, you shouldn't have tried to run away like that on me. I told you not to run, didn't I?" He leaned closer to me I could smell his cologne it smelt sweet with a hint of spice his breathe smelt minty it was scaring me on how detailed my senses have become.

I was frightened and started to cry. I had no idea what was going on and he wouldn't tell me anything. I didn't know who he was or what he wanted. Another vehicle passed and in the beam of the headlights I saw to my alarm that the driver was Tyler, the man with the angry dog. I didn't even know what to think after that, all I could ask is why?

"Tyler?" I asked in shock as I crossed my arms and looked out the window passing lots of trees that were blowing like mad in the wind, I could see tons of deer in the ditch.

"Yes Liz I will explain later, but we will talk some more when we get to where we going," Tyler replied as he shifted the truck into drive and started heading up the road.

"How come I couldn't recognize your voice I mean you I have a British accent?" I asked as I stared at him waiting for his response.

"I do talk with an accent my dear, but I had to learn to speak without one," Tyler explained as he quickly looked at me.

"So where is Zeus, your dog?" I asked.

"I left Zeus at home so he wouldn't get in the way of things," Tyler replied as he turned on the high beams to see the road.

That explains why his truck smelt like dog and also why the seats where all torn up in the back. My mind was exhausted from all the thoughts I rested my head against the window and closed my eyes. I must have fallen asleep because the next thing I remember is Tyler shaking me to wake me up.

"What do you want, go away I am trying to sleep," I said pushing him away.

Tyler was annoyed and took me in his arms and carried me inside. I opened my eyes a bit just to enough to see where he was taking me. I was way too exhausted to even try to fight. I noticed he was carrying me inside a small log cabin at a small lake surrounded by trees. It was an older cabin, inside there was an old stove and a loft where he had his bed. He lowered me carefully on the bed and waited. When I finally woke up and realized I was inside a building I shot straight up, and looked around I was so disoriented. I got up and looked down over the railings to see if I could see Tyler. I climbed down the ladder and ran out into the living room I ran right into Tyler.

"Well, love, you are awake I see. Now go get into a change of clothing. The bathroom is over there," Tyler said pushing me toward the washroom he then threw a nightgown at me. I stood at him strangely holding the nightgown in my hand.

"Why do you have a women's night gown?" I asked looking at him with a weird expression.

"It was my mother's. We spent a lot of time growing up here," Tyler explained. "Go on, do as I say." Tyler said as he turned around and left me be so I could change.

Why is he so pushy? I unravelled the nightgown. It is a pretty purple color with black lace at the bottom it was very pretty but he expects me to wear this. The washroom was tiny. I kept banging my elbow into the wall as I struggled out of my clothes. There was a constant drip-drip-drip from the old faucet. It smelt like mold in the bathroom I needed to get out of there before I passed out from the smell. If it is true about being werewolf the intense smells suck I can smell the slightest smell and times that by 100 and most of the time it was disgusting smells.

I put the night gown on and washed my face. I took a deep breath and opened the door. Tyler was standing in front of me.

"You scared me!" I yelled at him as I shoved him aside. "By the way you might want to do something about the mold in the washroom it is unbearable," I hissed as I stormed away heading for the ladder back to the room.

"Is someone crabby?" Tyler asked and followed me into the bedroom.

"Yes I am, because you won't tell me why you kidnapped me and why you are making me wear this," I snapped back at him. I turned away from him and climbed the ladder up to the loft and flopped down on the bed.

"I will explain everything in the morning just get some rest, Liz," Tyler replied as he laughed at me.

I pulled the covers over me and lay there but I couldn't sleep. I got fed up with not being able to fall asleep, so I got up and climbed down the ladder. This was kind of an annoying set up, I mean up and down this ladder constantly. I peeked around the corner just a bit I could see into the living room, the living room was fairly big with a fire place in the left corner he kept a pile of wood right beside it I noticed that the sofa that was a brown color, he had an old orange shag rug. I saw Tyler standing over by the window and I could hear him speaking on the phone with someone but as soon as he saw me he quickly hung up.

"What do you want?" Tyler asked, annoyed by my interruption.

"I am thirsty and I can't sleep," I replied and sat down on the couch with my arms crossed.

"Well I will get you a drink," Tyler said and headed towards the kitchen. He brought me a glass of water.

"Thanks." I said as I took the glass from his hands I took a couple sips and set the glass down on the counter beside me. Tyler looked at me funny but he didn't bother asking why I asked for a drink when I wasn't really thirsty.

I could see that he was staring at me intently. It was creeping me out I sat in silence on the couch. Tyler suddenly got up and grabbed my arm then threw me into a spare bedroom next to the washroom it was a small room, barely big enough to fit a double bed and a dresser. The walls were covered with paintings all of them were wolves. They were beautiful. I started rubbing my arm I couldn't understand why Tyler was being so rough.

"What the hell Tyler! Couldn't you ask me instead of hurting me?" I shouted at him through the half-open door.

"Oh you're a big girl, besides you're supposed to be tough now not wimpy. Start acting like a wolf," he snapped back.

I ran out towards him in the living room and pushed him on to the couch, our faces almost touching. "How the fuck, do you know I am a wolf?! I didn't even know I was a wolf." I yelled at him as I pinned him down, determined not to let go until I had an answer.

"That's a girl. I knew you had anger in you, love, and your eyes just went yellow." Tyler pushed me away and threw me onto the floor.

"You still didn't answer my question! I want to know how did you know?" I asked as and got back on my feet totally ignoring the fact that he just said my eyes changed color that wasn't really my concern right at that moment.

"I said I would explain everything to you in the morning, now get to bed!" Tyler shouted at me, and I noticed his eyes they turned a green colour when he got mad.

"No!" I yelled and sat back down on the couch, angrily.

Tyler lifted me up and carried me into the bedroom and threw me on to the bed.

"Liz you are so stubborn. I am going to stay in here until you fall asleep," he said and laid on the bed next to me.

"If you would just explain it now then I could my mind to ease," I replied as I faced the wall.

"There is too much to cover," Tyler said as he moved closer towards me.

I noticed him slowly moving towards me but all I could think of was how my life was changing and I didn't know how to deal with it I didn't know what to expect. I started sobbing, I then turned onto my back and quietly spoke up.

"Tyler what is happening to me?" I asked him, tears running down my cheeks.

"I guess I will tell you since you won't wait until tomorrow. You were given the gift to turn into a wolf," he replied as he wiped the tears off my cheeks.

"Are you one?" I asked him, fighting back a yawn.

"Yes, now go to sleep," Tyler replied as he started to doze off.

"One more question, how did you know I was one?" I asked him turning my head towards him.

"I could smell you," Tyler replied closing his eyes.

"Oh," I was too exhausted to ask any more questions I dozed off.

I woke up to find Tyler cuddling with me. He was snoring. I could see on my phone that it was only 5:30. I put down my phone and tried to wake him up. Tyler moved a little and I tried to ignore his snoring but it was too much. This bed was too small and it was too hot in the room. Finally I kicked him off the bed. That woke him.

"What the hell Liz!" Tyler yelled as he got up on the bed again.

"Well stop snoring," I replied laughing at him.

"I am sorry, but you didn't have to kick me off the bed," Tyler snapped back already halfway asleep. He put his arms around me again and he was really close to me, it was starting to get uncomfortable the heat was getting me sick.

"Why are you so close to me Tyler?" I asked as I moved a little bit away.

"Because I like cuddling with a pretty wolf girl," Tyler replied bringing himself closer to me.

"Alright then," I answered back with a grin on my face.

Finally dozing off again my phone alarm went off and it scared the shit out of us both. I grabbed my phone to see the time and it was noon.

"What time is it Liz?" Tyler asked me as he stretched.

"Noon," I replied and crawled out of bed.

"What!" Tyler yelled as he jumped out of bed and went flying out of the bed room.

After struggling to get dressed in the small bedroom I headed into the tiny washroom to clean my face off thinking about what Tyler told me last night, about us being werewolves. I was still in shock I couldn't believe it, I mean how can I believe it werewolves they don't exist. Banging on the bathroom door caught my attention.

"Hurry up in there we have a lot to discuss today," Tyler said banging on the bathroom door.

"Okay, okay. I am coming," I said opening the bathroom door. Tyler stood there waiting for me.

"Are you hungry?" Tyler asked as he sipped on a cup of hot coffee.

"Yeah I am and I wouldn't mind a cup of coffee," I replied as I followed Tyler into the kitchen.

The kitchen was small and it was painted a tan color. The fridge was an olive green. His whole cabin smelled like a giant tree inside.

"So can I have a cup of coffee?" I sat down pouting at the kitchen table.

"Help yourself Liz," Tyler responded and moved so I could get myself a cup from the cupboard just above the sink.

I grabbed myself a cup of coffee and for some reason anything I did, anywhere I went, Tyler was always there staring at me. He started to frighten me. I tried ignoring him but it's almost like he doesn't trust me, probably because I did try and run the first time but I was scared out of my mind.

"Why do you always stare at me like that, Tyler? You make me feel uneasy," I asked as I sat back down to enjoy my cup of coffee.

"Because for one reason I don't trust you, for another I find you extremely attractive," Tyler answered and poured himself some cereal.

I didn't know what to say, I was surprised. I just kept drinking my coffee and would look at him occasionally.

"Are you going to eat?" Tyler asked as he put his bowl in the sink and went into the living room.

"Yeah I will." I replied as I made my way to the cupboards and poured myself a bowl of corn flakes. Kind of boring I thought to myself pouring the milk. I went and sat in the living room next to Tyler.

"Liz the next full moon is a couple of days away I want to teach you what to expect," Tyler said and moved closer to me as I sat there listening, twiddling my thumbs. I didn't really want to hear what he was going to tell me because I still don't want to believe that I was a werewolf. It seemed like a horror movie I was trapped in and hopefully I would wake up from it.

"Okay. So, Liz, when the full moon hits, you're going to feel pain because your bones are shifting. Once you shift a few times it won't be so bad. You're going to feel stronger and all your senses will be heightened even more than ever. I know you are asking yourself why I kidnapped you. Let me tell you. I did it because I knew you wouldn't believe me so I had to take control of the situation. This was the only way I could help you. I hope you understand the predicament I found myself in," Tyler explained to me as he got up from the couch to put another log in the wood stove.

"Yeah, I mean you are right, I probably wouldn't have come with you but when you explain it like that it sounds comforting, I still am having a hard time believing this I mean how did you react when you found out you were a werewolf?" I asked between sips of coffee. Looking around the living room I noticed a huge painting hanging about the fire place. It looked like wolves fighting humans. I was amazed by this painting the details in it were amazing it looked so real. I kept staring at it until Tyler started speaking again.

"Like you, I was in denial until the full moon came and the curse was triggered. I have been looking for more werewolves ever since without ever seeing one. Until I came across you. I couldn't risk losing you. I hope you will understand one day," Tyler explained as he walked to the front door to put his shoes on.

"I guess I kind of understand. But are you going to keep me locked up here forever? I do have my own life, like school, friends, and my own house." I asked as I got up and headed for the kitchen placing my bowl in the sink. I stood there leaning against the counter.

"No I am not going to keep you here forever, just until the full moon is gone. I didn't really kidnap you. I am here to help you. I don't want you to be by yourself in all of this. It is scary. Come outside, I want to show you around," Tyler was already in his jacket and he opened the front door.

"Okay, I guess," I said, putting my coffee cup down, I got my jacket and shoes on and we went for a walk around the beach. He brought me through a path in the forest nearby. It was windy but the sun was shining, I could hear the birds whistling.

"This is where my brothers and I use to wrestle when we were younger," Tyler pointed out to a spot on the ground which formed a small mound.

"How many brothers do you have?" I asked tripping over mound.

"Be careful. I have 3 brothers and 1 sister," Tyler replied catching me before I fell.

"Thanks. Where are they? Are they like you?" I asked as I took a deep breath in smelling my surroundings. The flowers gave off a very strong scent and the wax off the trees smelt sweet. I could hear and see all the bees around me moving from one flower to the next it was so beautiful. "No, they are something else and they live far away. I have not seen them for years," Tyler replied and took a quick look at his watch.

"What do you mean, 'something else'?" I asked.

"Let's head back to the cabin," Tyler said, ignoring my questions and we turned around to head back toward the cabin.

"What is that painting about in the living room?" I asked as we walked side by side. "My mom was an artist. That painting is about werewolves fighting amongst vampires," Tyler explained.

"Vampires! They exist to?" I asked looking up at Tyler.

"Yes, and they are bad," I could tell he wanted to drop the subject of vampires. Whenever he answered a question he was vague. He didn't want to continue the conversation. Then, as we were about halfway back I heard howling in the distance. I froze and looked up at Tyler.

"What it's just a pack of wolves, nothing to be scared of," Tyler replied as he nudged me forward to keep moving.

"They seem so close, though," I said. Finally we were back on the dirt road again.

"You don't have to be scared of them. They can sense you," Tyler said as he reached into his pocket to pull out his keys.

"That is cool I suppose. What are we having for supper?" I asked as I took off my shoes and jacket and sat down on the couch in front of the wood stove.

"I was thinking some steaks and potatoes," Tyler replied as he slipped his shoes and jacket off and headed in the kitchen to prepare the food. . I sat in the living room but I started to feel light headed and I got up wash my face in the bathroom. As I looked in the mirror I could see my eyes had changed to a gold colour. I screamed and ran out of the bathroom.

"Liz, what is wrong?" Tyler asked his arms open to hug me.

"My eyes turned a gold colour. Is that supposed to happen?" I asked. I couldn't control my shaking I was so scared.

"Yes, Liz, you will notice a lot of changes happening in the next couple of days." Tyler was busy with the steaks and potatoes which were now ready to be barbequed.

After we were done eating I took a shower. I started to feel light-headed once again so I leaned against the shower door and waited for this uneasy feeling to pass by. Once the full moon had passed would I be able to return to my so called "normal" life? The full moon was in a few days and I needed to be prepared for changes that were about to happen to me. I didn't know what to expect and I have never been so scared. I got out of the shower and brushed my teeth and my hair and put back on the nightgown. I went back in to the living room and sat down in the living room.

"Do you want some hot chocolate?" Tyler asked and sat beside me.

"Sure." I moved closer to him.

"So how long have you been a werewolf?" I asked Tyler as he prepared the chocolate.

"All my life, but didn't find out until I was 18." He handed me a mug of steaming hot chocolate.

"How did you find out?" I asked as I blew on my hot chocolate.

"I was a typical teen I liked to party and fights always involved me. This one particular fight was when I found out something strange was happening," Tyler replied as he stared outside watching the trees blow in the wind.

"Well can you tell me?" I asked.

"It's too long of a story, but basically I lost all control and murdered the young teen I followed him home and attacked him in the forest nearby. When I was attacking him he pulled out a small knife and stabbed me in the stomach I was bleeding but when I lifted my shirt up to check out how bad the wound was I noticed it heal almost instantly, that freaked both of us out. At that point I was even angrier than before and I couldn't take any chances of this boy staying alive so I finished him. I don't like to talk about it I was a monster until I found out ways to cope with it," Tyler explained as he stared blankly outside.

"Oh I am sorry I was just wondering," I said feeling uneasy.

"That is ok you didn't know. Besides I don't blame you for asking questions there will be a lot more questions some will come unanswered. Anyways dear we better get to bed," Tyler responded as he placed his cup on the counter and headed towards the washroom.

I got up from the couch and glanced outside. It looked so beautiful out there so soothing. I to placed my cup on the counter next to Tyler's and headed to the bedroom and crawled into bed. Tyler joined me soon. With a long two days ahead of us and I wanted to have enough energy. It was time for bed but I couldn't sleep. I lay there staring up at the ceiling. I rolled over to see if Tyler was asleep. I nudged him to see if he would wake up and all he did was groan and turn over. I laughed a little to myself and closed my eyes and trying not to let my mind race with too many confusing and exhausting thoughts. The next thing I know I am being shoved off the bed.

"Ouch! What the hell Tyler?" I shouted as I picked myself off the floor and glared at Tyler.

"It is time to get up, Sleeping Beauty," Tyler replied as he laughed at me.

"Well I am glad you got a good sleep and ready for the day, I am going to climb back to bed and sleep for a little longer. Unlike you I didn't sleep." I whined as I climbed back into bed.

"No, you have to get up. We have a long day ahead of us," Tyler replied and pulled the covers off the bed and threw them onto the floor.

"No! Go away!" I shouted and curled myself up into a little ball on the bed but before I could react Tyler picked me up and threw me outside onto the muddy ground. I landed with a thump. It hurt.

"There now, you have no choice but to get up and get ready," Tyler said and closed the door, waiting for me to come barging back inside. I had something else in store for Tyler, though. Instead of going back into the cabin I climbed up tree and hid. I waited for him to notice that I wasn't coming back in. He slowly opened the door open and came outside.

"Where are you? I know you haven't gotten too far you don't know your way around here!" Tyler shouted. He was close to the tree now. I stifled a laugh and I leapt out of the tree and landed on top of him.

"What the hell?" Tyler asked as he got up from off the ground, wiping the mud from his pants.

"Well you honestly think I would let you get away with what you did? Throwing me in mud? Yuck! I had to get you back somehow." I wasn't sure what he would do next so I walked back into the cabin. The look on Tyler's face was priceless it made me laugh even more. Tyler had made a decision. He came running back inside and lifted me in his arms and threw me onto the bed.

"You want to be like that? I can play to," he said and started to tickle me.

"Tyler no, I hate being tickled, stop it!" I yelled. I kicked him in the shins. Then he finally stopped and, breathless, we stared into each other's eyes for a few seconds. He kissed me and I kissed him back. Before I knew it we were taking our clothes off and making love. It felt amazing to be with him, I mean he was just like me. And he was attractive and funny. I loved the feel of him touching me. It felt so right. His hands were all over me and mine all over him. I had never felt so good in my life being close to him made me feel alive somehow. He then proceeded to undress me his hands still wandering all over my body. I pulled his shirt off and then we gave each other a couple of kisses. I didn't know what came over me but I wanted him so bad. We then took off the rest of each other clothes and he started kissing me all over. He then ripped off my panties with his teeth. I then laughed "boy you are part wolf". His 200 pound frame then got on top of me as he thrusted himself in and out of me it felt so good I didn't want it to end. It lasted for quite a while, he then kissed me a couple of more time and then we lay there, in silence, staring at the ceiling. I was waiting for him to say something in the silence that was becoming too awkward.

"Wow, that was amazing," Tyler said with a big smile on his face. "But we should get up now, I have some stuff I need to tell you so you can be prepared for tomorrow." Tyler got off the bed.

"Yeah, I know." I said as I continued to lay there.

"We should practice fighting," he said. "And jumping and then do some laps around the lake," Tyler suggested as he buttoned his shirt. I looked at him funny kind of funny.

"Why?" I asked confused. "I mean I am not complaining at least you're not like most men and fall asleep after making love," I said giggling.

"Most of the time I do, you caught me at a time where I can't fall asleep there is too much to teach you. You need to start preparing yourself for the future. There are bad people out there and if they find out about you they will stop at nothing to capture you. You need to be able to defend yourself in this world. People won't understand what you are," Tyler explained. I watched him as he ran outside, climbed up a tree and jumped down, landing on his feet.

"Alright, I suppose you have a point," I replied. I stared at the roof of his cabin. I was looking to see if I could actually jump that high. I closed my eyes. Well here goes nothing, I said and jumped up onto the roof of his cabin. That was so cool! I just jumped about 12 feet without injuring myself. Maybe I should play in the NBA I thought, laughing to myself

"Good job. Now see if you can catch me," and Tyler took off.

"That's not fair you got a head start," I complained as I jumped down from the roof and started running after him. I stopped to smell the air around me. I could smell everything and I could hear and see every little detail. I heard noises come from the bushes I could smell Tyler hiding in there, I smiled as I darted towards the prickly bushes and jumped on Tyler's back.

"You're a brat. How did you find me?" Tyler asked, laughing.

"I followed your scent and you had to hide in the prickly bushes didn't you?" I asked with a smile.

"See there you go, you can track down anything. Now, let's go back inside I will tell you what you should expect as far as physical changes are concerned." Tyler said as we headed for inside the cabin.

I sat down on the couch and Tyler got the wood stove going. As the flames grew he said "First of all, just about an hour or so before the full moon you will feel pain in your stomach. You will get light headed and everything you look at will appear blurry. You will have the urge to tear everything apart. And then you feel weak until you are completely transformed. When you are shifting you will feel and hear your bones crack and break. You will feel your hair grow all over your body. Your eyesight and hearing will be altogether different." Tyler explained as he looked toward his mother's painting in the living room.

"Now, I am even more anxious and scared than I was when I first learned I was a werewolf," I replied and took a deep breath in. "What if I hurt people? I can't live with that guilt," I asked as I covered my face with my hands and leaned further into the couch.

"I know it's very overwhelming but you will get used to it, though, as you shift more and more. Anyway we should call it an early night." Tyler said as he headed for the washroom.

I nodded and got changed into the nightgown and waited. Tyler finally came out and I went in the washroom and stared at the mirror and looked at my teeth to see if they were sharp which they weren't, yet. I brushed my teeth and splashed water on my face. Okay, Liz, you are strong. Just keep thinking positive. This will be over with soon. Oh, who am I kidding? I am changing my body into that of a wolf. How much positive thinking can I actually do? I closed the washroom door behind me and crawled into bed with Tyler. All I could think was tomorrow was the big night the full moon. What was really going to happen to me?

Chapter Two

THE FULL MOON

I woke up to the sound of Tyler getting ready for the day. I could barely move I was so tired. All I wanted to do was sleep some more. Who was I kidding? I knew that wasn't an option.

"Wake up, Sleeping Beauty," Tyler said to me as he threw my clothes at me.

"Just a couple more minutes," I turned over to try and go back to sleep.

"I don't think so, missy," Tyler took me in his arms, carried me into the living room and threw me on the couch.

This week has turned out to be a nightmare I just wanted sleep so bad. Today was the big day getting ready for the full moon tonight. Every time I thought about it my stomach would get queasy. Why me? I kept asking myself over and over again but no one could answer it for me, not even Tyler. From the kitchen I could smell bacon. Tyler was busy with the frying pan. I looked over at a brown woven laundry basket sitting by the wood and noticed some of my clothing folded nicely inside the hamper.

"Tyler, you washed my clothes for me, thank you," I told him.

"Someone has to do the woman's work around here," he said, laughing.

I sat down at the kitchen table, waiting for the coffee to be done brewing.

"We're having eggs, bacon, and hash browns," said Tyler reaching for the plates.

"Sounds good," I said licking my lips thinking about enjoying the hot coffee he had also prepared.

"So, are you ready for tonight?" he asked, licking bacon grease from his fingers.

"Not really. Do we have to lock ourselves up like they do in all those movies?" I asked looking at all the food he had put on my plate.

"Yeah, I have a cellar that I use I will show it to you later." Tyler was obviously hungry. His plate was almost empty now and I was still picking away at my food Tyler then got up from the kitchen table and put it in the sink.

I didn't say anything. I stared at the food, poking the eggs with my fork. I somehow wasn't hungry anymore. But I knew I should eat in order to have energy for tonight. I slowly ate the breakfast that Tyler had so thoughtfully prepared. It took me forever. I looked over at him and I could see he was concerned.

"Are you okay?" he asked, busy washing the dishes.

"I guess, considering I am about to change into a wolf. Yep I am just peachy," I said sarcastically. As soon as I said that I heard a muffled knocking at the door. I ignored it thinking it might be the wind but the knock got louder.

"Tyler, there is someone at the door!" I shouted at Tyler as I got up from the kitchen table and made my way past the door into the living room and sat on the couch.

"I am coming!" said Tyler as he looked out the window to see who it might be. He couldn't make out who was there so he went to the door and opened it.

There were two of them both were wearing suits their 6 foot 200 pound frame could barely fit into.

"Sorry to bother you, sir, but you're going to have to come with us," said the one with brown hair as his brown eyes stared at Tyler as he grabbed him by the wrist.

"What the hell!" Tyler shouted as and managed to push them outside. He managed to close the door and locked it behind him.

"What is going on Tyler?" I asked Tyler, anxiously. We heard a loud crash and constant pounding on the door, soon the men barged through the door and stabbed Tyler with a syringe. The brown hair guy grabbed him and the other guy who had short blonde hair just looked at me with his blue eyes. You could tell he wanted to do bad things with me.

"Grab the girl Vince," The brown haired man said to the other man with short blonde hair as he lifted Tyler up to bring him outside. Due to the substance found in the syringe Tyler was left unconscious.

I couldn't move.

"Now, sweetheart, are you going to behave? Or do I have to knock you out too?" The blonde hair man asked as he grinned I could see the syringe ready in his hand.

"No I will behave. I need my shoes." He kicked them toward me and I slowly put them on. Who were these men and what did they know about me and about Tyler? They could be in for big surprise. They shoved Tyler in the back of their white van and told me to sit in the passenger side.

"Hurry up Curtis we have to move," Vince yelled.

"I am Vince," Curtis snapped back.

"Where are you guys taking us? What do you want form us?" I asked, struggling to sound calm as we started to pull away.

"You will see," Vince answered with a very serious look on his face.

I had no idea where they were taking us but it seemed an endless journey. I stared out the window looking at the open fields. I tried to talk to them but they just ignored me. We took a sudden turn toward an old looking motel. It was grungy and ran down. They parked the vehicle and I stared at the motel and cringed.

"Get out. We are staying here for the night," Curtis said as he got out of the driver's side.

I didn't argue, I unbuckled myself and hopped outside. It was getting dark now and I could feel a strange pain in my stomach. The two guys looked at each other and smiled.

"It is starting," Vince and Curtis said as they looked at each other and grinned.

I ran to Tyler to try and wake him but there was no response. Vince came over to me and grabbed me by the arm and took me into the main part of the motel to check in. In the meantime Curtis waited with Tyler until the room was unlocked.

"The room is for four adults?" the clerk asked as she reached for the keys. I noticed her name was Lisa she could barely see over the counter and her long blonde hair covered her blue eyes.

"Yes, and it will be charged to my credit card," Vince answered back handing the clerk his card.

"Thanks. Your room is 202, have a good night," Lisa said and smiled as she handed over the keys.

He then shoved me towards the room and followed very closely behind me so I wouldn't try anything making it back to the room meeting Curtis and Tyler at the door. Curtis picked Tyler and we unlocked the door. Curtis then tossed Tyler onto the bed. I just sat on the bed next to Tyler hoping that he might wake up. Suddenly, a sharp pain hit my stomach and I fell to the floor screaming in agony.

"Make it stop!" I screamed. My screams woke up Tyler right away he started holding his stomach as well.

Tyler said "Everything is a blur! Liz, are you there?" Tyler asked as he curled up into a ball.

"Yeah I am, Tyler. Are you alright?" I crawled closer toward him trying to make it back onto the bed but I was so weak I just sat on the floor with my knees tucked under my stomach.

Vince came close to me and I felt a sharp sting as he stuck the syringe into my neck. I screamed and fell over as the pain stopped. Curtis went over to Tyler and did the same thing. Tyler sat up and looked over at me he looked so worn out. I struggled to get up slowly and went and sat beside him on the bed. In the meantime Curtis left the room, a few minutes later he came back with a huge crate in his hand it looked like an oversized dog kennel. I didn't bother asking what it was because I assumed it was for Tyler and me.

"Who are you people?" Tyler asked, staring at Cutis and Vince.

"That is none of your concern. What is your concern, though, is that we know what you two are. There are people out there who are looking for you two," Vince stated as they started setting up a cage. Just as I thought a huge dog kennel it was big enough to fit at least three large dogs, it was black in color and the bars were very thick made out of steel. Finally I decided to ask the men what they were planning on doing with that cage.

"What are you doing with that cage?" I asked moving closer to Tyler as I put my hand on Tyler's leg.

"We are putting you two wolves in here. The stuff we injected into you will only suppress your transformation for a while," Curtis explained as they grabbed us and pushed us in the cage. I huddled in the back right corner I was petrified Tyler sat down beside me he held my hand.

"Tyler, I am scared this isn't how I wanted to do my first transformation," I whispered as we just sat in the corner of the cage.

"I know Liz, me to. Just relax everything will be alright I am here with you to." Tyler answered.

Soon the pain started again, we were both screaming in pain. I looked up at Tyler and his eyes were now yellow and his teeth had changed shape. They were now pointed and sharp. I could hear our bones cracking and I could feel my legs bending and my face stretching. I looked at Tyler he was now a wolf and my own sight was so different that I knew I had also shifted. We paced back in forth in the cage growling our two captors. My vision was so different, I couldn't really see color it was very strange.

"Look at how beautiful the girl is. She is pure white. It seems to me those wolves are getting along quite well," Curtis said to Vince as they just watched us. Tyler and me just sat there we started howling soon we laid down on the floor of the cage we eventually fell asleep.

The next morning we both woke up, but now back in human from. I didn't remember anything from last night. The cage door was wide open, and that was when I realized I was naked. I screamed and tried to cover myself up the Curtis threw me some clothes I grabbed them and put them on. Tyler woke up soon after I did, and Vince threw him his clothes to.

"So are we allowed to go back home now?" I asked them as I got out of the cage.

"No, sweetheart, we have something else in store for you two." Vince and Curtis said as they both laughed and got ready to leave the hotel room.

My whole body ached and I was starving. To my surprise I realized that my libido was through the roof. I wanted Tyler. My need was urgent. I kept staring at him. I wanted to make love to him so bad what a horrible feeling, being a wolf it's intense.

"We're leaving we have very little time," Vince said.

Tyler and I waited by the door and watched the both men take the cage down. Once they were finished we followed them outside back to the van, Vince opened the trunk up and placed the cage inside. Curtis got into the driver's side, Vince closed the trunk and walked around to the other side and opened the side door for us.

Tyler and I sat in the back together. Vince got in the passenger's side as the vehicle started and we were on the road again.

"Tyler is it normal for my libido to be so intense right now?" I asked him.

"Yeah it is," Tyler answered and placed his hand on my leg.

We stopped at a restaurant to eat, thank god because I was starving. It was only fast food, but that didn't matter at this point.

"Excuse me, but I have to go the washroom now," I said to the men and I gave Tyler a look that signalled that I wanted him to come with me and I left.

"May I be excused as well?" Tyler asked as he started to stand up to leave the table. "Alright but I will stand out the washroom door so you can't try anything stupid," Vince answered as they both stood up and headed for the washroom. Tyler walked faster so he could use the same washroom that I was in.

I stood there waiting for Tyler soon the door flung open Tyler came bolting in I grabbed him and pushed him up against the wall and we started kissing. Tyler's hands were all over me. Then his pants were came down, and then mine too. He inserted himself into me and I moaned. It felt so good for the short time it lasted. When we were done and had fixed ourselves up I left first. I walked out of the washroom and saw Vince standing there he was reading a paper I ignored him walking right past him.

"I am finished we can go back to the table," Tyler came out as he walked back to the table Vince drew his eyes away from the paper and started walking behind Tyler. After everyone had finished eating we all got back into the van and we drove off.

"Liz we have to get rid of these men, I want you to bite the one in the passenger side I will bite the other man that is driving," Tyler whispered in my ear.

I slid closer and we sat pretending everything was alright. We gave each other the signal I lunged forward and bit Vince's neck he screamed in pain leaving Curtis to panic causing him to swerve off the road into the ditch. Vince was bleeding from the neck and Curtis hit his head pretty hard on the steering wheel they were both unconscious. Tyler and I got out of the vehicle, Tyler went to the driver's side he opened the door and pulled Curtis out leaving him on the ground. I went around to the passenger's side I opened the door and yanked Vince out also leaving him on the ground. Tyler got in the driver's side and I hopped in the passenger's side, we sped away. The van had a bit of front bumper damage but nothing too bad so we decided to steal it to get us to a different location.

"Why the hell didn't you bite him like you said" I snapped at Tyler.

"You were too quick" Tyler replied

"Bullshit", I laughed "You were just too scared" I said as I teased him and started nudging him.

"Yea, yea, yea whatever" Tyler smirked.

"I wonder what those men really wanted with us." I asked, hoping that maybe Tyler knew something.

"I am not sure, but I didn't want to stick around to find out," Tyler replied.

As I stared out the window all I could think about was last night, and how strange everything has become. My whole life is changing so fast.

"So are we boyfriend and girlfriend now?" I asked Tyler as I yawned.

"If that is what you want, love. I am all over the idea," Tyler said as he turned and smiled at me.

"I want that. I wasn't sure if you did," I replied as I smiled back at him.

"Of course, baby, how could I not want that. You are sexy, smart, funny, and you're a wolf like me," Tyler said as he stared at me. He then stated to rummaging through the center console to see if he could find anything useful and found a cell phone he turned on the GPS to figure out where we were.

"Are we going to stay in another hotel tonight?" I asked Tyler.

"Probably," Tyler replied, studying the tiny map on his phone.

It was a long drive and all I wanted to get some sleep and cuddle with Tyler. We pulled up to a hotel with a sign outside saying it had a pool and a hot tub. The hotel was your average hotel it was a couple stories tall nothing too fancy. They had a room available so we checked in and the first thing we did was to relax in the hot tub. My body was so sore after a night trapped in a cage and not to mention that my bones just broke and shifted into a wolf form.

"This feels so nice," I said to Tyler as I leaned over the bubbling water and kissed him.

"I know, baby," Tyler replied as we started making out in the hot tub. We had to be careful as other guests might come in at any time. Deciding that we were getting too hot from the water we made our way out of the hot tub and made our way back to our hotel room, where we got undressed and had a shower together.

"You have such a nice body," Tyler said as he explored my body with his fingers.

"You do too," I replied feeling running my hands up and down him. The water from the shower running down our bodies we stepped out of the shower and dried off. We finally flopped ourselves on the bed. We were both exhausted. Tyler was holding me in bed and I think I fell asleep instantly. The next morning I woke up and I felt so good, I got out of bed and turned on the coffee maker in the room. I heard Tyler and yawn and I knew he was awake I glanced over at him he just laid there with his eyes wide open.

"How did you sleep last night?" I asked as I waited for the coffee to brew. The coffee machine was loud as it perked the coffee steam ran from the machine I could tell it was going to be strong I could smell it.

"Okay," Tyler answered. He got out of bed and leaned over to kiss me on the neck.

"I slept fantastic," I replied pouring a cup of coffee and taking my first sip on the not-very-good coffee. I made a disgusted face and stared at the thick sludge that was supposed to be coffee. Tyler looked at me funny.

"What is wrong you look very disgusted?" Tyler asked as he proceeded to get dressed.

"This coffee is too strong," I replied as I shrugged my shoulders and still drank it anyways.

"You're still going to drink it?" Tyler asked he scratched his head.

"I guess so," I replied as I drank it as fast as I could without burning my mouth. I finally finished and set my cup down by the coffee machine.

"How about we go down to the restaurant and get you real cup of coffee," Tyler suggested as he put his watch on and combed his hair. I nodded and quickly brushed my hair and threw on some different clothing.

Downstairs in the restaurant I looked at the menu but had a hard time deciding.

"Hello, my name is Tracy and I will be your waitress. Can I start you two with anything to drink?" Tracy asked, pen and paper out. I studied our waitress she was short and stalky with short brown hair with blonde streaks she wore a lot of bright coloured eye shadow. I noticed her nails to be painted a bright pink colour.

"I will have a coffee." I said.

"Me to," Tyler replied.

"Okay, I will be right back with your coffees," Tracy answered.

"So what are you having?" I asked Tyler.

"I am having eggs and bacon. What about you?" Tyler asked me.

"I am having a whole wheat bagel and a fruit cup," I answered back.

"Here you two go, what can I get you two for breakfast?" Tracy asked us getting ready to write it down.

"I will get bacon and eggs, I will have my eggs easy over," Tyler replied.

"I will have a whole wheat bagel, toasted with butter on the side and a fruit cup please," I replied.

"Ok," Tracy replied as she picked up the menus.

"So do you think we are safe?" I asked Tyler as I put cream and sugar in my coffee and stirred it.

"I don't know," Tyler replied as he took a sip of his coffee.

"You don't eat much do you Liz?" Tyler asked as he inhaled his food.

"I haven't been hungry the past few days," I replied as I buttered my bagel.

Tyler looked over my shoulder and saw two men in suits standing in the lobby, he quickly looked away.

"Liz there are two men standing over there, I think I know who they might be. They are dressed the same as Curtis and Vince. They haven't seen us yet but we have to get out of here," Tyler whispered and looked around to see if there was a way out without them spotting us.

"Shit there was no other way out," Tyler hissed as he grabbed my hand and we ran past the two men. Of course they noticed us and they quickly took after us.

"There they are, go after them before they get away!" The taller man shouted as they chased us.

"Did I mention the part where after you have had your first transformation you can turn at will," Tyler shouted to me as we kept running.

"No, how do I do that?" I asked. Tyler looked back and saw they were still chasing us.

"Just think about being a wolf," Tyler said. I looked at Tyler and soon he was on all fours he was too fast for me at this point I needed to do the same.

So I stopped running, thought about it and then I was on all fours running to catch up with Tyler. We ran and ran until we finally lost them. We then ran back to the hotel and shifted back into human and we stole some towels from the pool area, then we rushed back to our room.

"Wow that was close!" I said to Tyler resisting the urge to throw him on the bed and make love to him as I got dressed.

"Too close. We need to leave," Tyler was already dressed.

We left the hotel. I don't know where we will be going next. It seems we are not safe anywhere. I still am in shock to think I am actually a werewolf. I thought they only existed in movies, but here I am running away with my boyfriend, who I might add that is a werewolf too. We are running away from God knows what. We got back into the vehicle and took off.

"We might have to go live with a pack of wolves," Tyler said to me driving fast but carefully so as not to attract police attention.

"You're kidding right? Please tell me you're kidding." I said as I shot Tyler a serious look.

"Well, Liz, I don't know any other options. We're not safe anywhere, but we need gas," Tyler announced and he pulled into the first gas station he saw.

"How are we going to afford our gas and we need clothing Tyler?" I asked.

"Maybe the men left money in here somewhere search the glove compartment," Tyler suggested as he checked the cup holders. I opened the glove compartment and there was a credit card stashed away I picked it up and looked at it.

"Here is a credit card probably for the company they work for," I replied as I handed the credit card over to Tyler. He took the card from me and looked at the signature on the back it looked like a bunch of scribbles.

"Ok this signature should be easy to copy I will give it a shot, do you want anything?" Tyler asked as he opened the door.

"Water please," I replied.

"Alright I will be back," Tyler replied as he stepped out of the van he filled the van with gas I saw him run into the store.

I noticed little driblets on the windshield and it is starting to rain. Great, just what we need is rain. Tyler ran back to the vehicle to avoid getting too wet.

"The card worked?" I asked as he handed me my water.

"Yep, but let's get out of here before they find out otherwise," Tyler answered as he started the ignition and we sped off.

"So where are we going?" I asked Tyler as I got the phone off of the center console to try and figure out where the GPS said we were. I opened my bottle water and took a couple sips.

"I was thinking somewhere on the west coast," Tyler replied and turned on the stereo.

"Is this what our life is going to be like, running all the time?" I asked.

"I don't know, Liz, I am just as frustrated as you are," Tyler changed the station.

"I know we both are frustrated and tired. I am just wondering how those men knew we were hiding the first time, and how did those men find us at the hotel. Something strange is happening and I have a feeling this is just the beginning. I wish I had some answers," I said to Tyler as I could feel a yawn coming on.

"I know I am really confused it's almost like they have been tracking us down for a while and just waiting for that perfect moment to catch us off guard," Tyler replied.

"Yeah that could be possible," I said as I laid back in my seat and closed my eyes. I must have dozed off because Tyler is now poking at me to wake me up.

"What?" I asked as I slowly tried to open my eyes.

"I need a break. I am pulling off to the side of the road because I need to have a nap," Tyler said as he brought the vehicle to a halt and shut the engine off.

"I have to go to the washroom," I said and went in search of private place. There was a ditch. I came back to the vehicle and I was freezing and wet from the rain.

"Will you lie down with me in the back?" Tyler asked.

"Sure," I replied with a smile.

We crawled to the back and Tyler was cuddling with me, and I was right up against him. I pressed myself against him to get warmer, I heard Tyler moan and he held me tighter. And then he fell asleep. I couldn't, though. I just lay there. I got up and stepped out of the van for a bit I walked around the ditch for a while it wasn't raining it was still cloudy out. I scoped the area to see if I could spot anything I noticed a couple deer not too far from where I was standing they looked at me and took off. I was starting to get chilled so I crawled back into the back with Tyler, starting to get bored I turned to face Tyler and I kissed him. Perhaps that would wake him up. Tyler opened his eyes and smiled.

"What time is it, love?" Tyler asked me as he stretched.

"It is 10:00 pm, you have been a sleep for two hours," I told him and kissed him again.

"Are you in the mood?" Tyler asked me and started kissing my neck.

"Now I am. What about you?" I asked him.

He put his hand on my breasts.

"It is really easy to turn you on," I told him.

"Ever since I first saw you I knew I had to have you. I couldn't stop thinking about you; you turn me on so much." Tyler replied slowly lifted my shirt up while kissing my neck.

"You turn me on too." I got on top of him.

"Oh baby," Tyler moaned and rolled us over so he was now on top and he started caressing me all over.

Tyler carefully removed each item of my clothing and I helped him to take his off and then he bent me over. "You're so hot baby," Tyler said. And he was in me.

"Tyler, harder," I moaned, my body electric with feeling.

There was something about Tyler that made him look evil, but it was sexy. This felt so wonderful it lasted for such a long time I never wanted it to end.

"Tyler, whatever you do, don't stop," I said and held him even tighter.

"I wasn't planning on it," Tyler said as he moved with even more intensity.

"Because I am about to have an orgasm," I said breathless.

"Wow, Liz, that just turned me on even more," Tyler said and moved faster and deeper and more urgently.

When Tyler had finished we lay in silence for a few minutes but it was cold in the van so we helped each other put our clothes back on and Tyler started the vehicle up again. I was sore but in a good way.

"Liz that was amazing. You are so sexy," he said as we drove back toward the highway.

"I know it was," I said, smiling.

"A few more hours and we will be in the mountains," Tyler said.

When we finally arrived at small town we pulled into the hotel It wasn't the nicest the lights in the sign was burning out and it seemed deserted but it had a bed and a pool and that is all I care about. We were both so exhausted we fell onto the bed. I just hope we might have a few days to relax before we have to start running again.

The next morning when I woke up for some reason I was freezing. I hopped in the shower and just stood there under the hot running water. I finally worked enough courage to get out and freeze. I got dressed, brushed my hair and just sat down on the bed and played some games on the cell until Tyler woke up. A few minutes later he woke up.

"It is freezing in here," Tyler groaned as he slowly got out of bed and made his way to the washroom closing the bathroom door behind him.

"I know it is," I replied as I was still playing games on the phone.

Tyler was still shivering when he came out and got dressed very quickly.

"What are the plans for today?" I asked Tyler and got up to blow dry my hair.

"I don't know. What did you want to do?" Tyler asked me as he kissed my neck.

"Maybe go for a walk." I said as I stared at myself in the mirror.

"Yeah we could," Tyler said as he grabbed me and guided me onto the bed.

"No, I am not done," I told him, but Tyler had me pinned and started kissing me, his warm breath on my neck. He stared intently into my eyes. "You're so beautiful Liz, I love you," Tyler said in such a sincere tone.

"I love you too." I said smiling.

We got ready and headed for the restaurant.

At breakfast Tyler suddenly said, "What do you think about living on the coast?" and took a sip of his coffee.

"That would be okay, but there's one little problem. All my stuff, everything I own is back in Prince Albert." I said as I shot Tyler a concern look.

"That's okay. We will go there and get a house, and then come back to Prince Albert and collect your stuff," he replied.

I didn't know what to think. Was this the end of our chaos or was it the beginning?

Chapter Three

THE NEW BEGINNING

On the way from Banff to Vancouver we saw a lot of moose, elk, and mountain goats. I couldn't believe how beautiful the mountains were, they were astounding. Although it was getting dark now I could still see everything just as clearly as if it were still broad daylight. I was staring out the window when all of a sudden I saw wolves, a pack of them, standing on the side of the road.

"Tyler there is a pack of wolves over there. They are standing there," I said pointing at them.

"That is normal. They can sense that we are here." Tyler replied.

"Wow that is too cool. Tyler do you think there are other were-wolves out here?" I asked.

"Probably, I just haven't had any luck finding any of them," Tyler replied and turned the radio up.

We were now driving through Kelowna. What a beautiful city. Vancouver was so far away it felt like forever. I nodded off to sleep and was woken up by lot of blinking lights and noises it sounded like sirens.

"Where are we?" I asked as I rubbed my eyes.

"Getting a ticket from the cops. I was going a bit too fast" explained Tyler and I laughed.

"No really where are we?" I asked looking annoyed.

"I just passed what looks like an accident but the sign up a head says we are about 60Km always from the big city," Tyler replied.

"Finally all this traveling is getting horrible," I said complaining as I tried to doze off again but I couldn't.

About half hour later I could see the lights as we were approaching the out skirt of the city. I was getting really excited I could feel butterflies in my stomach.

"Guess what! We are in Vancouver now! Look!" We quickly found a hotel, a nice looking one for a change. So we pulled in and went to see if there were any rooms available. Luckily there were so we checked in and got into our swimming gear right away and headed down to the pool. Tyler picked me up in his arms and threw me in the pool.

"Tyler you ass! It is cold!" I shouted at him though I couldn't help but laugh.

"You're a wimp," Tyler said as he jumped in and started to splash me.

"Don't you think you have tortured me enough," I said. I dove under the water and pulled at his trunks.

"Hey! I don't think so," he said and started swimming away.

"What? I wasn't going to do anything." I swam towards him, slowly.

"Pulling down my trunks in a pool where anyone might come in is nothing? Yeah right, love," Tyler climbed out of the pool and headed for the hot tub.

"Wait for me," I said.

The heat was so nice I felt I could fall asleep right there. We sat in the hot tub and began to relax. I stared at Tyler and his cute face and smile. I moved closer to him and he put his arm around me and he held me. After a while we both agreed it was getting late and we had a long day ahead of us so we got out of the hot tub and headed Back to our room, before falling asleep we talked for a bit we cuddled and fell asleep.

The next morning I got up and started getting ready for another day of figuring out what to do. I managed to snag an elastic band from the front desk and put my hair up in a bun. I really hated living without all my hair supplies, make up and clothing. I looked at Tyler he was still sleeping I just laughed to myself and I turned on the t-v. I started flipping through the channels I stopped at some cartoons laughing to myself I noticed Tyler lying there with eyes slightly opened, he slowly woke up and made his way towards the bathroom. I just continued watching TV.

"Good morning, sleepy head," I said with a sexy grin.

"Mmm, good morning sexy," Tyler said jumped on the bed he sat behind me and started to kiss my neck. I closed my eyes and smiled I turned around to face him putting my arms around his neck and kissing his lips.

"So what are the plans for today?" I asked after kissing him.

"I thought that we could go and look around at some houses, maybe do a bit of shopping" he replied.

"Ok, that sounds good but with what money?." I asked looking concerned.

"We can use that credit card we just won't get anything too expensive until we can make it back to my cabin, I have money stashed away there for emergencies," Tyler explained.

"Alright I guess we have no choice because I need clothing," I replied.

We both were ready to go, we didn't have a clue were to start.

We drove around aimlessly looking for a realtor business, and after driving around for two hours we finally came across one. There were a 4 weeks until the next full moon so we still had lots of time to get prepared. We parked and got out of our vehicle and went in.

"Hello, can I help you two?" A tall slim lady with long black wavy hair asked us.

"Um yeah, we are new to Vancouver and we were looking at houses, can you show us anything?" Tyler asked her.

"Yeah sure I can, my name is Sarah and I can show you around." And she did. Sarah took us to 5 houses that day Tyler and I agreed on one certain house, they were asking $480,000 for it. We looked around and this house was amazing, it had two full baths and a bathroom attached to the master room, it had a huge basement and a pool in the back yard. The back yard had a couple pine trees and a perfect area for a garden then I noticed I could hear the ocean from where we were it was such a soothing sound.

"Do you like this one, Liz?" Tyler asked.

"Yes, I do it is gorgeous," I said and hugged him.

"Thank you Sarah we will get back to you on an offer later until then take care," Tyler thanked her as he shook her hand.

"You're welcome and if there is anything else I can help you with please don't hesitate to call me," Sarah replied as she waited for us to leave so she could lock up.

"Well dear we can't exactly make her an offer yet I need to get back to my cabin so I can put that money into my bank account then we can come back to Vancouver and make her an offer, until then we will just have to jump from hotel to hotel until we can make it back to Prince Albert. I am sorry you have to live your live like this I just wanted to help you out I didn't know other people knew about our existent I would have been more prepared and careful," Tyler explained as we walked to the van.

"Honey its ok you didn't know. I know you were just trying to help," I replied as we sat in the fan for a few minutes figuring out what we were going to do. We both decided on some lunch so we headed to the nearest restaurant.

Stopping at a small dinner I asked Tyler, "So when are we going to go pick up my stuff from Prince Albert?" I asked as we sat down and scanned the menus.

"Soon," he replied as he looked around the dinner waiting for a server.

After eating we drove around the city for a while. I had never been to Vancouver and it was so pretty. I was looking forward to walking along the beach and swimming in the ocean. How I loved the ocean. I wanted to go and visit Sea World too.

"So where did you want to go?" Tyler asked me as he took a quick look at the time on the radio..

"Can we go to the beach?" I asked with a smile.

"Yeah sure," Tyler plotted the details into the cell phone to find how to get there.

We finally made it to the beach and I was so excited. As soon as I saw the beach ahead of me I ran towards it.

"Catch me if you can!" I shouted at Tyler as I stripped and kept running.

"Okay!" Tyler shouted back at me as he ran trying to undress himself to.

I was not expecting it, but Tyler ran up behind me and tossed me into the water, Tyler jumped in with me.

"I win," Tyler said smiling at me.

"You cheated," I said kissing him.

Tyler and I just swam in the water it was so beautiful the water was so warm and the waves were coming in peacefully, all the seagulls were screaming away the sun was so hot I felt so relaxed I was hoping that Tyler and I could stay here forever and never have to run anymore. We then got out of the water and sat on the beach to dry off. What would I say to my friends and family back home, though? I don't think I could tell them that I am a werewolf and my boyfriend who kidnapped me is a werewolf. This is not going to turn out well. How could I explain that this all began with Zeus's collar and how it ended up in my place?

"Tyler, how did Zeus's collar end up in my place?" I asked as I picked up some sand and sifted it through my hands watching it pile back onto the ground.

"One day I went over to your place to see if you were home and I noticed that your door was unlocked. I let Zeus in to sniff around because I wanted to make sure that I was right about you. I guess when I heard you come home we both bolted out of there and Zeus must have got his collar caught on something," Tyler moved a little closer.

"Can't you smell me though?" I asked.

"Yes, but I just wanted to be sure," Tyler put his arm around me.

"I see," I said as I noticed the sun starting to go down the sun set was amazing.

It then started getting dark so we decided to head back to our hotel room we got into the van when all of a sudden the cell phone started to ring.

"What should we do?" I asked "If we answer it they'll know we're not Vince and Curtis and if we don't they will think something is wrong." I explained.

"Just let it go to voicemail," Tyler said.

As soon as the phone stopped ringing Tyler picked it up and went into the voicemail and listen to what it was all about. The voice on the other end said "We found the werewolves, call me back as quick as you can." Then whoever it was hung the phone up.

I asked Tyler, "That doesn't sound to good does it?"

"No it doesn't it sounds to me that there are spies everywhere we go, they know where we are at all times," Tyler replied as he clenched the steering wheel in frustration.

Finally pulling to the hotel and making our way to the room Tyler started sniffing the air. I looked at funny we got to our room Tyler suddenly stopped and growled. He started sniffing around. He could smell something in the room. He seemed angry and scared at the same time.

"Tyler, what is wrong?" I asked as I started sniffing the surroundings to see if I could smell anything different. I had no idea what I was sniffing out.

"Someone or something has been here," Tyler replied and started to pace back and forth.

"What do you mean something?" I asked as I gave Tyler a strange look.

Another werewolf, or a vampire," Tyler replied and sat down on the bed.

"Wait a minute, did you say vampire?" I asked as I paced the room having a mini panic attack.

"Yes, Liz. We are not the only monsters on this earth. I told you back at the lake that you needed to be prepared for other beings. Vampires are one of them. I wasn't kidding when I said vampires existed." I tried to take in what Tyler had just said and he went to the washroom. Vampires? Before I could flinch a hand was over my mouth.

"Move you little bitch and I will break your neck! Do you understand what I am saying?" A man said to me as he pulled me closer to him.

I was so scared I just nodded my head. I didn't know what to do I could feel my eyes tearing up.

"You sure are a pretty little thing," The man said to me smelling my hair. I knew this man was tall because he was kneeling down so he could keep my mouth covered. His build was strong just by the way he held onto me.

I looked over and there was another shorter man with blond short hair stood there waiting, he moved to the washroom door so he could catch Tyler off guard. His blue eyes glanced at me as he was waited for Tyler. Tyler came out of the washroom and the man zapped Tyler a few times with a stun gun until Tyler fell to the floor the blonde haired man grabbed Tyler and dragged him on the bed and tied him up so he couldn't escape. The man that had me in his grasps just hung on to me as tight as he could I could barely breathe. I eventually worked up enough strength and I elbowed him in the stomach. He threw me across the room and fell to the floor holding his stomach.

"You bitch! I am going to kill you!" The tall man said as he got up and moved towards me.

"I wouldn't if I were you!" I said yelling at him as my eyes turned a golden colour and I growled. I scoped him out he ran his hands through his brown short curly hair his brown eyes glared at me.

"Holy shit, you're a werewolf?" The tall man said and backed off.

"Yep, and so is he," I replied as I pointed to Tyler still tied to the bed, and smirked.

"We're not scared of you two. We're vampires," the vampire that had been torturing me replied.

"Hmm, and now that you know we are werewolves are you going to leave us alone?" I asked as I stepped closer to them.

"Hah! Are you kidding? We like to torture mutts," The shorter vampire said laughing.

I just stood there glaring at them I went and ran over to Tyler to see if he was okay.

"What did you do to Tyler?" I asked, glaring at them.

"Oh nothing sweetie just a few zaps to knock him out," The shorter vampire replied smiling at me.

"And why didn't you zap me then?" I asked.

"Because you're a cute little wolfie besides, I needed someone awake to torture." The tall vampire replied. "By the way, sweetie, my name is Roman and this is Derek." Roman said introducing himself and Derek to me.

"Well Roman what are your plans for us?" I asked, so scared I was shaking.

"Oh, baby, you will see. We won't be too rough, that is unless you try anything stupid," Roman said as he grabbed my arm with a lot of force.

"Ouch," I yelped, trying to get away from him.

Roman increased the pressure on my arm. He was not going to let me get away from him. He was breathing on my neck and started licking it. I was disgusted and terrified at the same time. If only Tyler would wake up. I kept looking at him.

"I should bite her now," Roman said, laughing.

"Please just let us go you don't need to do this!" I yelled as I tried to escape I just kept grinding against Roman.

"No you two are coming with us, our master wants to see a werewolf for himself and we are not going to let him down, And I am enjoying you squirm like this," Roman said as his hands all over me now.

"Have it your way," I said as I turned around grabbed Roman by his neck and threw him against the wall I stood there for a couple seconds I didn't have much time to react then it hit me.

What if I were to turn into a wolf and scare them? It was worth a shot. I looked up at Derek and growled I looked over at Roman I strutted towards him kicking him in the side.

"You bitch!" Roman shouted as he slowly stood up holding his stomach.

"I told you to let us go!" I growled as I could feel the adrenalin move through my veins.

"What are you going to do about it?" Roman asked as he was about to back hand me. I stopped his hand and twisted it.

"I will show you," I replied as I let go.

Looking up at Roman I snarled, my fangs were showing and my eyes were a golden colour.

As I leaped towards him shifted now into a werewolf I jumped on him and almost bit him. I was just about to sink my teeth into his neck, when he grabbed my muzzle and held it tight causing me to back and shake my head. Roman then stood up and ran towards Derek. I stood there baring my teeth.

"Holy shit Roman! They can shift anytime they want," said Derek.

"We should get out of here," Roman said as they slowly started to back towards the door. They were walking backwards they didn't want to turn their backs on me. Keeping their eyes on me I then jolted and leaped on to Derek biting his thigh before they made it out. I could hear him scream all the way down the corridor.

I shifted back before doing anything I threw on the first thing I saw which happened to be one of Tyler's shirts I then proceeded to run to Tyler I cuddled up beside him and started to cry. After what seemed like an age I could feel Tyler begin to move.

"Liz, what happened?" Tyler asked, confused and groggy.

"We were attacked by vampires and I had to shift to chase them away," I explained and closed my eyes.

"What?" Tyler asked as he struggled to get up.

"Vampires, Tyler," I crawled under the blankets to feel safe once more.

Tyler said nothing. He looked at me and I could see he was worried. He pulled the blanket up and came into bed with me.

"Are you okay? Did they hurt you?" he asked and put his arm around me.

"Yeah, I am okay, I am little shaken up. One of them threw me against things," I replied.

"Fucking vampires! Did they ... touch you?" Tyler asked in a way where I could tell he really didn't want to know but he was concerned.

"What do you mean?" I asked as with a confused gesture.

"Like anything sexual," Tyler replied as he touched my face.

"Yeah one of them tried" I said.

"I hate them. They will repay" Tyler said as he held me tighter.

After a moment's pause, he kissed my neck.

I loved his accent and every time he spoke I would melt. I pushed my hips against him really hard. I loved to hear his reaction when I did that.

"Why do you do that?" Tyler asked as he rubbed my shoulders.

"Because I know that it turns you on." I said as I smiled a bit.

"It does turn me on, sexy girl," Tyler said as he kissed my neck, his hands on both my hips now.

I turned to face him and our bodies locked. But we were both so tired and frightened we ended up falling asleep. I remember checking the time when I woke up suddenly. It was 4 a.m. I pulled the blankets up around my neck when I heard the door of our room fly open, as if it was being pulled off its hinges. The noise startled us and we were both instantly awake. I turned on the light next to the bed we were sleeping in.

"Who's there?" Tyler asked, nervously looking around the room.

"Well, well if it isn't the werewolf couple," A voice replied back as he appeared out of the corner.

"Tyler it is Roman, that vampire that was here earlier," I whispered to Tyler.

"You bitch! You bit Derek and now he is dying. For that I should torture you until you beg me to kill you." Roman said with anger in his voice.

"You touch her and I will rip your throat out!" Tyler yelled and growled at the same time.

"That is very amusing. You really love this girl?" Roman said with a big grin on his face. He walked closer to us.

"Do you want me to bite you too?" I asked him. I stood up and my eyes turned a golden colour.

"Not if I do this first," Roman said and pulled out a gun with some kind of red colored darts loaded in it. The last thing I remember is Roman laughing and me and Tyler blacking out.

When I woke up my head was pounding and I had no idea where I was. Slowly I realised I was locked up in a cold cement cell there was spider webs in every corner of the cell and the dust was causing me to cough. I started looking for Tyler but there was no sign of him. I crouched in a corner and cried I was scared and frustrated and angry. I heard laughter and footsteps approaching.

"Well, I see my wolf girl is awake," Roman said with a smirk. I looked up at him disgusted by him he was so evil.

"I am not your wolf girl," I muttered but loud enough so he could hear.

"Oh, honey, we will see about that," Roman said and unlocked the door of the cell. He pulled me out of it and I was still so weak I couldn't fight back. I was also hungry. Roman took me by my arm and led me up some stairs. Upstairs was so bright it hurt my eyes this house was different it didn't have a kitchen or a living room it was one big room with a bar in one area some seating, a pole to dance on and loud music I was covering my ears, the scent was disgusting, I knew the room was filled with vampires because I could smell them. They became still and stared at me. I couldn't hear what they were saying due to the loud music. Roman brought me into a small room where another vampire was. I looked around at his office and there were papers everywhere. He had paintings of vampires hanging all over the walls. The smell was disgusting, like sweat and cigarettes. I looked carefully at the vampire and got goose bumps. He smiled at me and continued talking on the phone. I avoided eye contact with him. After he hung up the phone he rose from his chair and approached me.

"Ah you must be Tyler's squeeze?" he said getting closer.

I nodded..

"How did you know his name was Tyler?" I crossed my arms.

"Because we tortured him before we locked him away," he answered with a laugh.

"You're disgusting," I snapped and I tried to bolt out the door but Roman stopped me and pushed me back towards the head vampire.

"Think what you want, sweetie. Let me introduce myself. My name is Damien and I am the head vampire. He then looked at the mirror on the wall and ran a comb through his black hair and asked Roman "'Does my hair look like it's graying to you?" as Roman let out a huge laugh. He then said "When I heard that there were two werewolves living here in Vancouver I had to see for myself and…but by the way, what is your name?" he asked.

I stood there petrified looking up at his 6 foot structure I couldn't help but think of how muscular he looked. His goatee ran against my cheek and sent chills down my spine. "My name is Liz. But what are you going to do with us?" I asked.

"Well, Liz, I am not sure yet what we are going to do with our pet wolves," Damien replied with a grin. I noticed that when he smiled he had dimples much like Tyler.

"If you're going to kill me, please make it fast," I begged as a tear rolled down my cheek.

"Oh Liz, I am not going to kill you. Not yet," Damien replied gently wiping my tear from my face.

"Where is Tyler?" I asked looking into Damien's brown eyes.

"Don't worry about Tyler. He is safe," Damien returned to his chair.

"How long are we stuck here for?" I asked as I crossed my arms in anger.

"For however long I choose. Now, Roman, take her away I have work to attend to."

Damien demanded.

"Let's go baby," Roman replied as he squeezed my arm again and shoved me out the door. He pushed me onto a couch and sat beside me, he moved really close to me and started smelling my hair. I moved away in disgust I then heard the office door open and Damien strutted out with a drink in his hand he then joined Roman on the couch. I thought oh great now what?

"Cut it out, man, I am sure this mutt doesn't like you smelling her," Damien said to Roman as Damien took a sip of his drink which I noticed was blood I could smell it.

"I really don't care what this wolf chick wants," snarled Roman and he started kissing my neck. It was all I could do but scream.

"Are you just going to waste your time with her?" Damien asked and then got up and moved around so he could come sit beside me on the other side of the couch.

"I am going to spend as much time as I can with her. I mean, come on you have to admit that she is a sexy wolf," Roman started running his hands up and down my body.

"Well yea she is, but we have stuff to do," Damien snapped back and stood up.

"I know but it can wait," Roman replied as he waited for Damien to leave.

"Whatever come see me in my office after," Damien replied as he walked away and started visiting with the others.

Roman grabbed me and led me to his room and threw me on his bed. His bed was queens size his sheets where a dark red color. His room was small the walls where black and all he had in his room was a bed, lamp, and a wooden dresser. He crawled on top of me and started kissing my lips.

"Stop!" I yelled at Roman as I threw him off me and he went flying into his dresser causing his lamp to fall off his dresser. I couldn't believe this was happening. I hoped it was a nightmare and that I would wake up next to Tyler on our bed in our hotel room. But I kept thinking this could be the end of my life.

"You stupid bitch, you like seeing me pissed off, don't you?" Roman hissed at me and jumped back on top of me, this time he wasn't so nice. He tore off my clothes and forced himself onto me. He pulled his pants down and forced himself in me. I tried not to struggle or to scream or to encourage him in any way. When he was finished I felt his teeth as he bit into my neck. Then I let out a huge scream, is this the way my life will end I thought to myself as I laid there frozen in fear.

Moons Tale

Chapter Four

PLANNING THE ULTIMATE ESCAPE

*R*oman walked out of the room leaving me lying on the bed bleeding from my neck. I realised later that I must have been unconscious. When I woke up, I slowly opened my eyes and began to wonder what had happened. I remembered with great embarrassment and anger what Roman had done. My body ached all over and my neck was still very sore. I worked up enough energy to move off the bed and managed to open the door. I knew I needed to be stronger than this. Come on Liz, I tried to give myself some encouragement. You are being weak you're a goddamn werewolf, after all isn't this time to start acting like one? I realised I needed to work on a plan in order to get me and Tyler out of this hellhole, but I needed more time. I moved off the bed and opened the door the music wasn't as loud as before so I could actually hear myself think. I stepped out of the room and closed the door quietly behind me I then turned around and ran right into Roman.

"Well, I see my little wolf girl is awake. Come and join the party," Roman said as he took my hand in his.

"This is the wolf girl. Don't you think she looks pathetic?" said a tall slim vampire lady who laughed in my face. Her rudeness pissed me off and I growled in her face and then turned around so I wouldn't have to look at her anymore.

"Be nice, Sally," said Roman, pushing her away.

"Yep, just as I though a weak little wolf," Sally said following me and determined to escalate the tension.

I turned around and pinned her up against the wall and bit her in the neck until she screamed and begged for me to stop.

"Now do you think I am pathetic?" I snapped back at her as I wiped her blood from my mouth. "You pissed off the wrong bitch!" I screamed at her as I watched her bite marks turn purple. She held on to her bite marks and walked towards me.

"You stupid bitch, I am going to kill you," she hissed as she stabbed me with a knife in the stomach, she then dropped to the floor.

"Think again, bitch. I just killed you," I said and laughed as I kicked her away, ripping the knife out of my stomach.

All the other vampires were watching. They were surprised that I had enough nerve to kill one of their own. Just as I was about to turn into a wolf something hit me in the back of the neck and I dropped to the floor. I was still conscious, but I was groggy, weak and confused.

"Roman, get her out of here now!" Damien shouted as he went over to look after Sally.

"Sally my poor girl. I am sorry there is nothing I can do to help you," he said as he wiped the tears from her face and without warning stabbed her in the heart to take her out of her misery.

"Where do you want me to take her, master?" I heard Roman asked as he picked me up from the floor.

"Take her to my office and sit her down on the couch I will deal with her," Damien said as he looked down at me with what looked like a sneer.

Roman brought me to Damien's office and dropped me onto the couch. "I feel sorry for you," Roman said as he kissed me gently on the lips.

Sometime later, I have no sense of the time Damien entered the room slamming the door behind him. He walked to the couch, picked me up and dropped me down on his desk as if I were a sack of potatoes.

"I am truly amazed on how strong you are, but you are no match for me, little girl!" Damien shouted at me as he pinned me down on his desk. He looked me up and down. "Hmm, but you're too cute to kill right now. It would be a shame. I am going to toy around with you for a bit first," he explained as he forced a smile.

"Just kill me and get over with. I don't want to be your toy," I hissed and spat in his face.

I could see the anger as he wiped the spit from his face. He lifted me up from the desk and threw me against the wall. I fell to the floor in pain. I was still trying to think of something I might do to get Tyler and me out of this hellhole. I could hear loud screams and tons of glass breaking coming from outside the door but I was still so groggy. Damien heard them as well and left the room to see what was going on out there. Before long he ran back inside the room and looked scared. He shut and barricaded the door.

"Your boyfriend got loose and now he has started killing my vampires!" he shouted as he moved toward me and picked me up. I have no idea where he was taking me but he had me over his shoulder and we were moving at an incredible fast speed. Moments later we went flying through a huge barricaded door, then up one flight of stairs and into a massive bedroom where he then tossed me onto a huge king size bed. I was sick to my stomach from moving so fast. The bed had a red canopy over it, he had a white duvet. I looked around the room the walls where painted a dark purple the window was tinted with red drapes, he had a massive closet with a mirror for doors beside the closest was another door I assumed that lead to the washroom and the floor was cement with the acceptation of a red area rug where the bed sat on.

"Now that I finally have you to myself I shall enjoy," said Damien as he licked his lips. He was sitting on the bed next to me.

"Get away," I snarled.

"Don't be like that, dear ," he said and moved even closer and started kissing my neck.

I pushed him away and ran to the door but he was too fast. He got there before I did, and he just threw me back onto the bed. He crawled on top of me and with his hands he started spreading my legs.

"Please, Damien don't I have had enough," I begged him.

"You're so cute and now you are begging me," he said as he pulled my underwear down and flash of pain took over my entire body. I tried to shut my mind off. I hoped that I might pass out.

"Tyler will find me and he will kill you," I hissed through the pain.

Still inside me, Damien just looked at me and slapped me across the face. I just lay there, sick of being abused by these blood-suckers. Disgusted with what just happened once again feeling embarrassed and ashamed and hateful. All I could think about was escaping and finding Tyler. I continued to block Damien out of my mind until he was done raping me. He was breathing heavily and in my face it smelt like cigarette smoke and blood. I turned my face and looked toward the wall and gasped for air. Damien then grunted and wiped the sweat off his forehead and rolled off me still breathing heavily. I slowly sat up and didn't say a word for a few seconds. I finally had enough with feeling grubby that I spoke up.

"Can I go clean up now?" I asked as I turned my head so I wouldn't have to look at Damien. God these vampires are monsters I thought to myself as I held back my anger and pain.

"Yeah, go ahead," Damien said as he rolled off me .

I got up from the bed and headed for the washroom that was attached to the master room. I turned on the taps and got into the shower. I was sore and tired I didn't know how much more of this I could take. I fell to the floor and cried. I let it all out. I was stuck here and Tyler didn't know where I was. I felt unclean. I knew as soon as I got out of the bathroom Damien would still be there waiting for me. I dried myself off and got dressed as best I could. I brushed my hair before I took a deep breath and opened the door. And there was Damien waiting on the bed, ready for more. He looked at me and smiled.

"How was your shower dear?" he asked, moving closer.

"Refreshing, I am now clean from you bloodsuckers taking advantage of me." I replied trying to back away.

"Now dear, don't be like that," he hissed and took hold of my arm and forced me back on the bed.

I needed to work up enough energy to turn into a wolf so I could bite him and escape this hellhole. One thing I didn't understand is why Damien was so much stronger than all the other vampires. I asked him what it was that made him stronger than all the other vampires. "You will soon find out, dear," Damien replied, and with a smile he was back on top of me. He starting kissing me once again and it sickened me. I wanted Tyler to find me so bad I just wanted to be close to him again.

"Can you please stop?" I begged him.

"No way, dear," Damien replied grinning as he kissed my neck.

I managed to throw him off and as I ran out the door I shifted myself into a wolf and I just kept running. I had no idea where I was going, but I just kept running. I ran into a forest where I saw a pack of wolves up ahead and I knew I would be safe there. I looked back but there was no sight of Damien anywhere. I blended in with the pack and the other wolves just sniffed me and decided to run off so I ran with them. I had no idea where we were going to go from here. I turned around and got a scent of Tyler being around, I looked around but didn't see anything except a lone wolf in the distance staring back at me. When the wolf saw me looking at it, it took off. I followed the wolf inside a dark shallow cave. The wolf shifted back into a human and yes, it was Tyler, I quickly shifted back to human form and hugged him. I never wanted to let him go.

"I missed you so much, baby," I squeezed Tyler and cried uncontrollably.

"I missed you too, my love," Tyler replied and kissed me reassuringly.

"Did you know that was me?" I asked, looking into his eyes.

"Yes, I did," he said, holding me closer.

"How did you know?" I asked.

"I could smell you, my love," Tyler said and held his hand to my cheek.

I was so happy I couldn't believe that I had found Tyler once again. I knew I never wanted to be separated from him again.

"We should get going," he said, shifting back into wolves as we had no clothing. Tyler then guided me away from the forest. We saw a couple people on some bikes we bolted towards them scaring them they screamed lost control forcing them to fall off their bikes. We stood there growling. They dropped their bags and took off running. Shifting back into humans we scavenged through the bags to find some clothing. I found a pink tank top, and a pair of purple leggings, Tyler found a plaid button up shirt and a pair of grey sweats. We quickly threw them on and headed back into town. We almost made it to our hotel when Damien appeared in front of us. He stood there, grinning. How did he know where to find us?

"Hello, you two. I knew you would be coming back this way eventually. It was just a matter of time," he said.

"Don't come any closer!" Tyler shouted as he took a couple steps back, and positioned himself between me and Damien.

"Oh don't be like that. I was just about to have some fun with your plaything when she ran away. What a shame." Damien waved his finger and took a step closer.

Tyler growled at him and just as Damien was about to grab me Tyler bit him violently on the arm. Damien froze in his tracks staring at his wound. He was shocked and couldn't believe what had just happened to him.

"You stupid ass! What have you done!" Damien hissed and crumpled to the floor in pain. He held onto his arm where the bite was already started to take effect. He glared at Tyler, cowered, knowing he was defeated, and ran away.

"I thought it would be harder to kill Damien," I said looking up at Tyler.

"I don't think I killed him. I think I just weakened him," Tyler replied and took my hand in his.

"Oh?" I replied. . What did Tyler mean by that? I thought a werewolf bite would kill any vampire?

"We have to get moving," Tyler replied looking very serious.

I had no idea what was going to happen next I just wanted to live a somewhat normal life. But here, we were on the prowl again, unsure what was going to happen next, not knowing where we might end up. Tyler seemed determined to get this fight over once and for all.

"Where are we going now?" I asked, trying to keep with him.

"I don't know," Tyler replied. But he eventually started to slow down as he realized he was going too fast. I soon caught up to him.

"So we are just going to keep running until we figure out where we go next?" I asked. I had to stop and clench my stomach. It felt as if someone had taken a knife and shoved into my stomach over and over again. The pain was intense and unreal. As I felt my eyes tearing up I started screaming as I dropped to the ground.

"What is wrong, Liz?" Tyler asked and ran over to me and crouched down beside me. He brushed my hair out of the way and wiped the tears from my cheeks.

"My stomach hurts. It's a sharp pain that won't go away!" I cringed in unbearable pain

Tyler picked me up and decided we need professional help. He took me to the nearest hospital where they rushed me into a side room and put in an intravenous and hooked up me up to all kinds of machines. I was so exhausted and in so much pain I passed out.

"Hello, my name is Dr. Grey, and you are the husband?" Dr. Grey asked Tyler as she glanced at her clip board.

"Um, no Dr. My name is Tyler I am the boyfriend." Tyler explained.

"Okay, Tyler. Can you tell me exactly what happened to Liz?" Dr. Grey asked.

"We were walking, she stopped and held on to her stomach and then she dropped to the ground she said it felt a stabbing pain." Tyler explained as Dr. Grey kept her eyes on Liz.

"Well, we will run some tests," Dr. Grey explained and started reading her notes.

Tyler sighed and when the Doctor left sat down on a brown chair beside Liz. He stared at her, wondering what could possibly be wrong. He could feel tears building up in his eyes as he feared the worst. What could be wrong with her? He kept asking himself. What if the doctors find out what she really is then all kinds of people will get involved. Soon Dr. Grey returned. She looked puzzled.

"Tyler, there is something really weird going on here. I mean Liz's blood tests came back all wacky. You need tell me what is going on in order for me to help her," Dr. Grey said, waiting for an explanation.

"I c…can't explain." Tyler stuttered and started crying. As much as he wanted to explain everything he knew he couldn't put our lives in any more danger.

"Well, Tyler. I am sorry I can't help then. We will just have to wait it out," Dr. Grey turned to leave.

"Wait!" Tyler shouted and reached for Dr. Grey's arm. "Let me explain," he said, shaking.

"Come into my office where it is private," Dr. Grey said and guided him into the room and closed the door behind them. She poured herself a cup of coffee and they sat down.

"Umm, well here is the thing Doctor, and I know this is going to sound weird, but Liz and I have been running away from vampires for about two weeks now. We have nowhere to go now," Tyler tried to explain.

"Tyler, I don't have time for these kinds of games. Liz has a serious medical problem and I need the truth," said Dr. Grey firmly and stood to leave the room.

"I am telling the truth, doctor. Liz and I are werewolves," Tyler looked her intently in the eyes and his eyes turned a golden colour.

"I see," said Dr. Grey. "So this might explain her blood work," Dr. Grey replied as she looked once more at her confusing notes.. "I mean that her blood work is so strange. Her red blood cells are through the roof and her temperature is higher than any human's," Dr. Grey explained as she nervously tapped at her clipboard. "Excuse me I will be right back," Dr. Grey replied as she pushed the chair away from the desk and sat up she headed out of the office and down the hallway. "Hello Hunter its Dr. Grey I found a couple of werewolves here in Vancouver the girl is in the hospital. What would you like me to do?" Dr. Grey asked Hunter over the phone.

"Don't let them go anywhere I will get Damien to kidnap them. Damien had the girl how does he always fuck up? Anyways good job we will take care of it," Hunter replied then hung up.

Dr. Grey then entered back into her office. Tyler was still sitting there in the same position.

"Well what do we need to do to solve this problem?" Tyler asked Dr. Grey. She turned and sat back down.

"I have to run some more tests," Dr. Grey replied as she took a sip of her coffee. "In the meantime I suggest you go and try to get some rest," Dr. Grey advised Tyler. He nodded and then left her office. He walked to the door that led to Liz's room and saw a black figure inside the room and crashed through the door.

"What the hell do you think you're doing?" Tyler asked the short stalky man who was busy with Liz's i.v. tube.

"Please, I am here to help, I know what is wrong with her!" the short stalky man shouted.

"Why should I trust you?" snapped Tyler.

"Because I am a werewolf just like the two of you now, please, help me! We need to get her out of here before Dr. Grey gets here" The short stalky man snapped as he shot Tyler a nasty look.

"Why what is up with Dr. Grey?" Tyler asked as he rushed to the other side of the bed and helped this man free her from all the machinery and tubes.

"I will explain later let's just focus on getting her out of here alive," Steven demanded as they struggled to carefully take the intravenous out of my wrist.

When they were finally done he carefully lifted her into his arms and searched for the easiest way out of the hospital without creating a scene. They made it outside and ran to the man's grey hatchback and then they drove off to his place which wasn't too far from the hospital, they got out quickly and ran inside. They set Liz down on a couch and then the man started mashing up some green and yellow herbs in a wooden bowl. Tyler said "This is no time to start making soup it smells like ginger and lemon."

The man says, "I'm not making soup you dumbass, I'm trying to save her life."

"Okay, can you explain to me what is going on?" Tyler asked him, hoping the man might answer. He was getting very impatient.

"In a minute, I just want to place these herbs all over her naked body," the short stalky man said as he took Liz's clothes off and sprinkled herbs on Liz's face, her stomach and her chest Tyler watched hoping Liz would soon wake up, he was so scared. He didn't want to lose her.

"What is this stuff?" Tyler asked the man and tried to make sense of these new surroundings.

"Your girl has been stabbed with silver. Probably by one of the vampires it is moving through her blood slowly causing pain and, unless we do something, eventually death," the short man replied as he started chanting some words.

"Fucking great! And all you're going to do is rub some plant shit on her and talk some gibberish that is so reassuring," Tyler said as he knelt beside Liz. "I don't even know your name I don't know anything about you." Tyler shouted as he sat there watching.

"My name is Steven and I live here in Vancouver, I am to searching for more of my kind. This herb that I am rubbing on her will draw the silver out of her body. And no, I wasn't praying, I was chanting," explained Steven

"Oh but how did you know we were here?" Tyler asked Steven and followed him into the kitchen.

"I could smell you two as soon as you walked into the hospital," Steven replied and poured himself a cup of green tea.

"Why were you at the hospital so late?" Tyler asked.

"I work there and when I saw your girlfriend getting admitted I waited for everyone to leave. I snuck into her room and that is when you came in and found me," Steven explained as he took a sip of his green tea.

"What is up with Dr. Grey?" Tyler asked.

"She is not to be trusted I have seen her hang out with vampires while I was working. She works with the vampires to get them what they want and in return she was to be turned," Steven explained as he looked over into the living room.

"Oh, well that explains why she wasn't really that shocked about Liz and I," Tyler answered back.

I opened my eyes but had no idea where I was. All I knew is that I was burning up and sweat was rolling down my face. I felt dizzy and weak. I had no idea what was going on and I could barely move. I saw that Tyler was with me and I could see there was another figure in the room he was shorter than Tyler I would say about a couple of inches shorter but about the same weight. He had the same color of hair as Tyler but I couldn't make out who it was.

"Liz, you're awake! How are you feeling?" Tyler asked me as he knelt down beside me. He gently kissed my forehead.

"Weak and hot," I answered.

Tyler helped me to sit up. "We already know you're hot," Tyler said as he helped me to sit up on the couch. Another man brought me a cup of tea.

"Thanks," I said looking at him. His blue eyes looked relieved.

"My name is Steven," he explained. "I am a wolf like the two of you. I was the one who saved you. You almost didn't make it." Steven replied.

"Thanks. What happened to me?" I asked as I looked around the room. It was very small and the white paint was chipping off the walls. There was a small TV with rabbit ears sitting on an old wooden stand. It smelt like spices and green tea.

"You were stabbed with silver. Do you remember being stabbed with anything?" Steven asked.

"Now that you mention it, after I bit Sally she stabbed me with a knife, I thought it was nothing, something that just rubbed my stomach." I explained as I tried to sit up but I was still in a lot of pain.

"You're lucky you made it to a hospital. You didn't have much time and it's a good thing I knew what to do," Steven said reassuringly and smiled at me.

"Thanks, but I need to clean myself up." I wiped the sweat that was forming on my forehead.

"Yes, of course" said Steven replied as he showed me where everything was.

I headed upstairs the stairs squeaked as I walked on them. I entered the bathroom it was really small just enough for one person at a time. The shower curtains were a baby blue color and where falling off the rings. I noticed a rust ring around the drain in the tub. I turned the taps on and ran by hand under the tap I enjoyed every second of that shower. I was so happy to be away from those dreadful vampires and happy to feel clean once more.. After I was done I dried off and wrapped a towel around me and went back downstairs. I could hear them talking about me and I stood there listening.

"Your girl sure is pretty, I wish I could meet a wolf girl," Steven said as he drank the rest of his tea.

"I know I am lucky. She means everything to me," said Tyler.

I could feel the tears building up and then falling down my face. I wiped them off and entered the room.

"Honey, I don't have a change of clothing." I said to Tyler as I held the towel on so it wouldn't fall down. I noticed Steven looking me up and down. Steven then went into a bedroom and came out with a duffle bag and tossed it to Tyler. He opened it and it had an assortment of women's clothes in it he then brought it over to Liz. Tyler then looked at Steven wondering why he would have women's clothing in his place.

Steven then said "I should explain, perhaps. They're my ex's. She left them here. See if there is anything that fits."

I thought finally I might have actually a clean set of clothes. I dug through the bag and took out a purple v neck shirt, and some blue dress pants I slipped them on they seemed to fit, a little snug but they will have to do. Tyler then went to the bathroom to clean himself up leaving me alone with Steven.

"So Liz, how long have you been a wolf?" Steven asked me as he stood up.

"All my life, apparently but I just found out recently that I was a wolf." I wanted Tyler to come back.

"It is too bad that you're taken, I would be with you in a heartbeat," Steven said as he reached out to touch my face.

When Tyler came back Steven pulled his hand away and I took the bag and went upstairs to rummage through it. I found a nightgown I could wear. I put it on and brushed my hair and my teeth and went back downstairs and sat on Tyler's lap.

"Hey, baby, you look hot and you smell sexy," Tyler said and kissed me affectionately.

"Can you guys do that in your own room?" Steven asked.

"Sorry, Steven, but she is so irresistible," Tyler replied with a coy smile.

"I know I would love to have her, but I see she is taken." Steven replied with a sad look on his face.

I felt sorry for him. He seemed so nice, and was caring and was certainly very attractive.

"You will find someone, eventually." I said smiling at him.

"Thanks, but I have been alone for a long time now and I have had no luck yet. Anyways everything you two need in the spare bedroom upstairs," Steven stood up and said he was going to bed.

"Ok thanks see you two in the morning," we said as he made his way to the stairs.

Tyler and I waited for as long as we could restrain ourselves before we raced each other up the stairs. The room had a double size bed with a brown comforter, there was a small white wooden dresser by the door, the window had bars over it, and the rug was a cream color and stained in some spots. Tyler sat down on the bed. He looked so cute. I went over to him and straddled him. He put his hands on my hips and pulled our bodies close and began to groan, quietly at first.

"Liz, I was so scared I was going to lose you," Tyler said as began kissing and breathing down my neck.

"I know, I didn't think I was going to make it either," I said. I leaned even closer to him. He lifted me onto the bed and his hands where all over me. I kissed him crazily I wanted him so bad. We made passionate love until we were so drained and tired we crashed.

The next morning I was startled by a loud noise. Something crashed downstairs. I reached for Tyler but he wasn't next to me. I went running downstairs to see what was going on but a hand grabbed me and yanked me into one of the other spare rooms.

"Shhh, honey it's me," Tyler said as he let me go.

"What is going on?" I asked as I kept my voice quite.

"Vampires," Tyler said as he pulled me closer to him.

"Where is Steven?" I asked.

"Steven is in here with us," Tyler whispered.

"What are we going to do you guys?" I asked quietly.

"We are going to have to transform and get the hell out of here," Steven said as his eyes turned a golden colour.

"He is right," Tyler said and was ready to transform.

We all shifted into wolves and raced downstairs. The group of vampires spotted us one of the taller more muscular vampires lunged at Tyler. Tyler dodged out of the way just in time for one of the smaller vampires that caught Tyler off guard and they went crashing over the couch, Steven turned around and leapt at a taller lady vampire that was ready to attack Tyler, Steven lunged at her ripping out her throat, Tyler got up as 3 vampires surrounded him and Steven. I jumped on the lady vampire's back biting into her neck blood poured down her body she screamed as she dropped to the floor Steven and Tyler lunged at the other two. Tyler pinned the muscular vampire to the floor he growled at him then proceeded to rip out his heart. Just as Steven was jumping at the stalky vampire he swatted Steven out of the air and Steven landed with a hard thud on the floor. The stalky vampire then lifted Steven up by the throat and hissed and opened up his mouth and was about to bite him. His teeth glistened.

I shifted back into human and yelled at Tyler. "Tyler his teeth are silver." Tyler then transformed quickly and noticed a piece of the broken couch and staked the vampire with the silver teeth. Tyler and I then shifted back to wolf form and all three of us took off outside.

We looked back to see if there were any other vampires following us and we ran. I was a little behind due to a hurt paw I received while fighting those vampires, then when all of a sudden something charged right into me and knocked me down. I shifted back into human form but I could barely breathe. I gasped for air and as soon as I caught my breath something kicked me in the side and I started coughing and holding on to my stomach.

"You stupid bitch, I am not letting you get away this time. You have caused me enough grief!" It was Damien. He yelled and grabbed me my hair and I screamed to see if the others could hear me.

"How are you still alive? We killed you!" I hissed at him trying to cover myself with my hands.

"You actually thought I was that easy to kill? Are you crazy, you foolish girl?" Damien picked me shoving me into his car. I sat there all curled up in a ball. I was naked still, having just transformed back to human and I didn't like the idea that my body was exposed for Damien to get a view of everything. He slammed the door shut and took the driver's side. He sat staring at me.

"Would you stop staring at me, please?" I shouted at Damien as I tried to open the door. He clicked the switch and it locked.

"Oh come on baby cakes, this is just the beginning. I know I will have so much fun with you," He started the engine and we drove away.

" I need to cover up." I shouted.

"Why would I want to give you anything to cover up that hot little body? Besides, I like what I see, sweetheart," Damien answered as he bit his lip.

I glared at him and turned away in disgust. I looked around intensely and I noticed a black and red blanket covering the backseat and so I used it to cover myself up. The drive was long and awkward I didn't know where he was taking me, but I knew it wasn't going to be my idea of a good time.

Chapter Five

THE NIGHTMARE

The car pulled into a long gravel driveway. The house was old and massive. Trees covered most of the yard, and vines crawled up the windows. It was like a house in a black-and-white horror movie. Leaves were blowing all around and there were a two more vehicles in the driveway.

"Well sweetheart, we're here," Damien said smiling as he climbed out of the driver's side and opened the rear door with a key. He pulled me out aggressively.

"Ouch! Can you be gentler?" I growled at him and I rubbed my arm. I held on to the blanket at the same time.

"Nope, but I will be rougher," Damien replied as he groped my ass.

He opened the door into a massive entrance. I could see a spiral stair case going up at least three floors. There was red carpet from the entrance and flowing right down the hallway and up onto the staircase. It was a beautiful home but I didn't want to be here. I wanted Tyler and Steven to come and rescue me. I had no idea if they even knew that I was missing. I could feel anxiety building up. I was so pissed off, frustrated and scared all at the same time. These goddamn vampires I finally escape and it seems I am back where I started. I wanted to know is how Damien survived that wolf bite.

"Hello, Damien you made it!" called a male voice as he stepped closer to greet Damien.

"Yes, Jeff, and I brought the wolf girl too," Damien replied and pushed me at Jeff.

Jeff pulled me closer to him. His 6 foot 200 pound frame held me tight, his facial hair rubbed against my cheek as his blue eyes stared a hole through me., his grip was so tight that I could barely breathe.

"I can't breathe," I said and started to squirm.

"That is just too bad, babe. You killed three of our vampires. Your boyfriend killed more than we can count. Someone has to pay the price," Jeff hissed and led me into downstairs into his yet another cold chamber, he threw me and some blue sweats and a white t-shirt they were defiantly men's clothing. I groaned in disgust as I put them on. Jeff smiled as he locked the cell doors.

"Please don't do this. I will do anything?" I begged as I ran my fingers through his blonde hair.

"Oh, babe, I know you will. You are so cute when you beg. You will do as we say regardless. You know, it is such a shame that were going to have to kill such a pretty little wolf. What a waste," Jeff laughed and kissed me on the cheek. He then went to talk to Damien outside the chamber I was locked in. I could hear their conversation.

"So Tyler, Liz's boyfriend, bit me but I survived. I guess that witch's spell really did work," Damien said laughing.

"That is awesome, I bet the looks on her face was priceless when you showed up again," Jeff replied. They laughed as they made their way back upstairs.

So he has a spell on him so he can survive a werewolf bite. How clever. I mumbled to myself as I sighed and slid down the wall onto the cold cement floor.

Meanwhile Tyler and Steven kept running, they hadn't noticed that Liz had vanished. They continued to run back to Steven's house finally making it back they shifted into humans and got dressed. "I think we lost them," Tyler said looking at Steven and looking around just to make sure.

"Yeah, I think so to, but where is Liz?" Steven suddenly asked.

"I am not sure. Liz? Where are you?" Tyler asked as he looked scoped the area.

"I think the vampires got her," Steven replied.

"No! Fuck! We have to find her!" shouted Tyler as they started back tracking to see if they might smell something.

Steven and Tyler walked for a couple hours, but had no luck at all. But they didn't give up. Tyler finally caught a whiff of something.

"Hey, Steven, can you smell that?" Tyler stopped to focus on what he could smell in that one spot.

"Yeah, I do. It smells like vampires," Steven replied as he looked up at Tyler.

They both shifted back into wolves and ran in the same direction as the smell. It was dark by the time they reached an old looking house. They saw roughly around four vampires walking around outside, Steven ran in front of them catching the vampires off guard, Tyler jumped on the smaller vampire biting down on his head blood dripping onto his face leaving him falling on to the ground he tried to get back but Tyler ripped out his heart eating it. Before the others could react Steven jumped on the taller male vampire impaling the vampire's head into a sharp rock sticking out of the ground. Leaving two vampires left, they got scared and took off in the other direction. Steven and Tyler looked around and shifted back into humans and stole the clothing from the dead vampires. They heard other vampires talking so they took off into the nearest bush to hide until they could come up with a plan.

Meanwhile I was sitting in the corner of this horrible dark cell, when I heard footsteps walking down the cement stairs.

"Get up, it's time for supper," Jeff said as he unlocked the bars. I just sat there motionless.

"Let's go woman," Jeff said as he pulled me up from the cement floor.

I took a step back from him but he reached for my arm and pulled me toward him.

"Don't try anything you might regret, doll face, because you won't make it out of here alive. Do you understand me?" He was whispering in my ear. I just nodded. "Good, now let's go eat," Jeff led me upstairs.

We went upstairs were the kitchen was and sat down at the dinner table, I was really shy I didn't say a word I just sat there listening to their conversation about how they enjoy hunting down humans and killing them, then there would be course of laughter I just picked at my rare steak and potatoes I didn't really want to eat anything.

"So this must be the wolf girl?" a tall well-built vampire asked Jeff.

"Yes this is Liz, our pet wolf. She will be staying with us for a long time," explained Jeff with a broad grin on his face.

Tears filled my eyes, but I couldn't help it, I ran away from the table and went and sat in one of the bedrooms I was a wreck. I knew they probably didn't like me leaving from the table but I needed to have time to myself. The room was smaller it had a double bed all made up with black and white covers, there was an end table beside the bed with a white lamp on it on the other side of the bed there was a little closet with no doors.

"Excuse me for a minute while I go fetch our wolf," Jeff said as he wiped his mouth with his napkin and took a sip of his wine before excusing himself from the table.

Jeff entered the bedroom and reached out and held me. I tried to fight him, but he was too strong.

"Leave me alone you blood sucker!" I snarled as I continued to struggle.

"Give it up, honey you're no match for me!" Jeff yelled and slammed me against the wall. He grabbed me and tossed me back down the hallway that led into the kitchen. I sat down on my chair beside Damien and crossed my arms.

"Welcome back, honey," Damien said with a chuckle in his voice.

"Don't even start with me," I snapped as I rolled my eyes.

"Someone is pissed off," Damien replied.

I was so disgusted with them I could puke, I wish a miracle would happen right about now then I heard a bang against the window I thought it was a tree branch banging against the window I glanced outside and saw Tyler looking into the window then he vanished again. I quickly looked away so they wouldn't notice me staring outside. I couldn't help but get excited.

"Can I go outside? I need some fresh air?" I asked Damien.

"Yeah, but I am coming with you," Damien replied as he led me outside. We were standing there when Steven hit Damien over the head with the end of a shovel Damien fell to the ground Steven dropped the shovel next to Damien. We then both took off running towards Tyler, not saying a word We ran and kept running not looking back to see if they noticed. No one was behind us, but we still ran until we reached a cave. I curled up against one of the walls.

"Liz, are you okay?" Tyler asked me as he cuddled up to me and kissed me affectionately on my neck.

"Not really, but I am better now that you guys are with me," I said kissing him back.

"We were really worried about you," Steven said as he went outside to see if there was any water nearby.

"Steven really likes you," Tyler said, a little nervously..

"Yeah, I can tell," I replied.

As soon as Steven came back into the cave I went running out side I wanted to look around that is when I came across a short waterfall that was crystal clear that poured into a nice looking lagoon, thinking it would be a good time to have a nice shower and swim. I thought about it and I figured maybe some other time I mean I was almost killed I need time to rest up.

I went back in to the cave and snuggled up with Tyler, Steven was already curled up snoring away. Tyler and I just laid there talking for a bit.

"Tyler I want to go back home," I said as I looked up and the rocky roof of the cave.

"I know and we will we just need to be careful where we leave our scent," Tyler replied as he put his arm around me.

We both eventually dozed off.

The next morning I woke up to the smell of coffee being brewed, I opened my eyes and looked around. I slowly got out of cave and noticed a bunch of campers a couple of meters away from us. They took off and left their stuff behind we were all hungry so we raided their stash and drank their coffee boy did it hit the spot. We looked around to see if we could spot any extra clothing just lying around. We went into one of the camper's tent and noticed some duffel bags we rummaged through them and found some clothing that will have to do. After getting dressed we needed to figure out what are next move will be. We had no vehicle though so we had to walk. Next thing you know it was lunch and everyone was starting to get hungry again we stopped at this roadside café we came upon. We sat down and looked over the menu.

"What are you having Liz, and please tell me you're having more than just a fruit cup and a bagel?" Tyler asked me with a serious look.

"No I am having bacon and eggs," I replied as I got my cup ready for the waitress when she came around.

"Hello my name is Tina can I start you off with anything to drink?" Tina asked as she got her pen ready. I was looking at Tina she was short maybe around 5"1 and she was chubby. She moved her brown curly hair out of her face her brown eyes were looking at us as she talked. I noticed her nails to be painted a bright red color she also was wearing bright colored eye shadow.

"Coffee," All three of us replied.

"Ok, and are you guys ready to order?" Tina asked us as she poured our coffee.

"Yeah I will get the bacon and eggs," I replied as I poured some cream and sugar into my coffee and stirred it.

"I will get a burger," Steven replied, as he took a sip of his coffee.

"I will get a bagel and fruit cup ," Tyler jokily said.

"Shut up," I said

" No I'm kidding Tina I'll have an medium all meat pizza" Tyler replied as he handed Tina the menus.

"Ok thanks," Tina replied as she took the menus.

"Did you guys notice anything odd about her?" Steven asked us as he took another sip of his coffee.

"No not really," Tyler and I both replied as we looked at Steven.

"Look at the way she walks and her scent I can tell that she is a vampire, we need to get out of here and quickly" Steven replied as he kept looking at her.

Our food came and we didn't make it obvious that we noticed she was a vampire, hopefully she didn't notice that we were wolves. She handed us our food and left without her saying a word we noticed her go to a phone and after she hung up about 15 minutes later about five vampires came through the door of the restaurant they were looking for us..

"Shit, we have to go!" Steven screamed as we bolted the other way we ran through the emergency exit causing the alarms to go off

"Get them!" Damien shouted as they ran after us.

We ran and we all shifted which made us too fast for them and we ended up losing them. We ran and ran eventually came to an abandoned cabin in the middle of the woods just on the outskirts of the city. We shifted and tried the door to see if it was unlocked the door had loud creek when we opened it, we went inside and searched all the rooms for some clothes. You could tell that this cabin has not been used for a while there was an old wood stove in the kitchen with a small wooden table and three wooden chairs that surrounded the table. The sink had a rust ring around the drain, and there was a large pot sitting on the stove. The living room had no rug only wooden flooring there was an orange couch with some rips in the arms and the back. I went to the bedroom it had a small bed with a wooden frame and a small brown dresser across from the bed, there was a few clothing that hung inside the small closet. The other bedroom had a bigger bed also with a wooden frame there was a bigger black wooden dresser beside the bed, the walls in the whole cabin were very bare no paintings or decorations of any kind. Tyler and Steven rummaged through the dresser and found some clothing after we got dressed Steven decided to use the washroom before we decided to leave. The bathroom was small it smelt like rotting wood the toilet was a green color and there was a gross rusty color that stained the toilet bowl the sink to had a dark right around the taps and the drain. Steven turned on the taps to wash his face the water stunk like sewer.

"Let's get the hell out of this dump," Steven said as we met up in the living room.

"Will we ever get rid of them? What do they want from us?" I asked the boys.

"I am not too sure," Steven replied. "They always seem to go after you, I think I might have an idea on what they want with you Liz," Steven said as he looked over at me.

"Why I would really like to know," I said sounding quite annoyed.

"They might be trying to create a hybrid half vampire and half werewolf, but don't my word up on that," Steven explained.

"That is disgusting," I replied.

"I know but it is the only logical explanation for all this," Steven announced.

"Ok can we just stop talking about this it is making queasy," I hissed.

"Sorry you wanted to know my thoughts," Steven apologized.

"I know I wish I hadn't asked. Anyways what are you going to do now?" I asked.

"We have to get as far away from BC and as soon as possible." Steven said.

"Great more traveling just what I wanted," I said sarcastically as we made our way to the bus terminal.

We made it to the bus terminal now looking at the dates and times our only closest choice was departing Vancouver in an hour the time was 5 pm and arriving in Edmonton tomorrow around 9am the next morning. We purchased our tickets and just hung out in the terminal waiting for our bus to arrive. I sat on the seat playing on my cell as Steven and Tyler were talking up a storm. Soon our bus arrived and we got on. We decided to sit at the very back so we could keep secretive. Steven and Tyler fell asleep and I just listened to my music for a while I eventually dozed off. We all suddenly woke up to a horrible noise that was penetrating our ears.

"What the fuck is that noise?" I asked the boys as we covered our ears.

"I don't know but it doesn't seem to be bothering anyone else," Tyler replied.

I looked around at the passengers then I came across a small boy with brown short hair playing with a whistle. It hit me this boy was blowing on a dog whistle. Now what are we going to do it's not like we can exactly tell that boy to stop he would know something was up.

"You guys that boy has a dog whistle," I said informing Tyler and Steven.

"Great I guess we will have to try and ignore it," Steven answered as we all put our ear buds in and listened to some music to cover up the horrible whistling sounds.

Finally arriving at our destination we got off at the bus terminal in Edmonton. It felt so good to get off that bus my legs were cramping and my ears were ringing.

"Wow what a long ride that was," I said as I stretched.

"Yeah no doubt, I just wanted to grab that whistle and chuck it," Tyler said as he rubbed his ears.

"I don't know about you guys but we should stop and get some clothing, then find somewhere to rest for the night," Steven said as he looked up the closest store to the bus terminal on his phone. "There is a store about 10 minutes from here," Steven explained as we headed out of the terminal and down the street. We went to the store and got what we needed and left. We didn't want to draw too much attention to ourselves so we were taking extra precaution.

Meanwhile the vampires sat around the table trying to figure out a plan to get Liz back.

"We need to get the wolf girl back!" Damien yelled as he threw a chair across the room and broke it.

"I know Damien, but how we don't know where they escaped to?" Jeff asked Damien as he sipped on a goblet filled with blood.

"I am going to have to get a hold of each and every vampire and tell them to keep an eye out for three werewolves and to kidnap the girl," Damien replied as he immediately got on the phone.

Meanwhile Roman stormed into the room. He was really pissed off.

"Roman, you're still alive?" Damien asked with a puzzled look.

"Yeah, I made it out before that psycho wolf could get me." Roman moved toward the couch.

"We keep losing the wolf girl, we need to find her," Damien said as he was talking on the phone.

"Do you know anything about the wolf girl?" Jeff asked Roman.

"Like what? I know that she has an attitude and she will let you know who is boss he knows how to play the cards right," Roman replied as he got up and poured himself a drink.

"I know we had her for a short time and she escaped, the next time we catch her we will have to watch her like a hawk, and the sexy part mmm I know she is fine," Jeff replied with a smirk on his face.

"If I catch her she will never escape again," Roman hissed.

"Okay, done. I asked all the vampires to keep an eye out for them," said Damien as he got off the phone.

"That is good. Hey, Damien, what do you think of the wolf girl?" asked Roman.

"I think she is attractive and smart, too smart." Damien poured himself a glass of red wine and his phone rang.

"Hello," Damien answered.

The voice at the other end said, "We found your precious wolf girl they are currently in Edmonton."

"Okay, good. Now kidnap the girl and bring her to Hunter," ordered Damien. He flipped his phone shut. "They have found her," he told Jeff and Roman.

Meanwhile we were trying to decide on what to do now. We decided on the West Edmonton Mall but again we needed to be careful there where vampires everywhere. Finally making it to the mall we entered in I was static I loved shopping. I bolted in the first store I saw that had purses and jewelry. The boys came running in after me looking pretty annoyed.

"Liz you can't just take off like that, you have to be careful," Tyler said as he shot me a serious look.

"I know I was just so excited I just didn't think," I replied as I reached for a purse to look at. It was a small hand bag with bright colors. I wanted everything. I didn't really want the boys to follow me because they would rush me so I made sure they were not looking and I took off to another store. It's not like they can't smell besides it's not like I took off very far, what is the worst that could happen? I asked myself as I looked at some wolf statues on a glass shelf.

I suddenly heard a voice behind me, "Can I help you?" I asked, uncertain if he worked there. I turned around there stood a fairly large man his hair was brown about up to his shoulders in length his brown eyes glanced down at me. He put his hand on my shoulder I noticed his nails to be painted black.

"No I am fine, now if you will excuse me I have to get going," I said as I started shuffling towards the exit.

"You're Liz, right?" the man asked and took a step closer.

"Who wants to know?" I thought this was a dangerous situation so I rushed out of the store.

" Damien warned me about you," said the man replied who followed me into the mall. I pulled away from him and ran. He wasn't far behind me, though. God he was fast.

I rushed around a corner and something grabbed my arm, I squirmed and kicked to defend myself.

"Don't fuck with me honey!" Another man hissed at me as he held me tighter, and brought me out the back doors of the mall where no one could see me. I managed to scream on the top of my lungs so Tyler and Steven could hear. The man that was holding me covered my mouth, but before they could throw me in the black van Tyler and Steven jumped onto the van. That is when I turned around to get a good look at my other kidnapper. He was tall well built his long blonde hair was covering his face.

"I wouldn't do that if I were you!" Tyler hissed as he shifted into a wolf and jumped on Bruce and ripped his limbs off, blood sprayed everywhere Tyler then turned to the other vampire and growled.

"Shit Bruce we should have thought this kidnapping out better," The blonde haired vampire snapped at Bruce.

"Yeah well we didn't Lenny," Bruce snapped back.

"Holy shit I am out of here!" Lenny screamed and ran the opposite direction of Tyler.

I fell to the ground and broke out in tears I didn't want a life like this where vampires were after me and attempting to rape me wherever I went. I wanted to die.

"How are we ever going to escape these stupid vampires?" I asked, still sobbing.

"How did they know we were here? Unless Damien has vampire friends here and asked them to look out for us," Steven said, looking up something on the phone.

"What are you doing?" Tyler asked him.

"I am trying to find one of my buddies on the yellow pages, his name is Hunter and he is a vampire, but he is a good friend of mine," Steven found the number and dialed Hunter.

"Hello, Hunter, it's Steven." As he talked he reached for a piece of paper and a pen.

"Can we meet somewhere it is important I have a couple friends with me, Tyler and Liz. They are also werewolves and there is something I must discus with you," Steven wrote down an address and time.

"You can come to the West side of the city by the West Edmonton Mall there is a small shack just nearby I will have a couple vampires escort you to my place within an hour," Hunter replied and hung up.

Hunter then picked up the phone, "Damien I'm meeting the wolves at my place in an hour. When would you be able to make it to my place to take Liz? Hunter asked as he looked at his watch. "In a couple of hours we already started driving a long time ago we knew Liz had made her way to Edmonton," Damien replied as he hung up the phone..

"We are meeting Hunter at the mall in an hour," Steven explained as he put the phone away.

"Are you sure we can trust him, I mean he is a vampire?" I asked shaking still from earlier.

"He is our only hope," Steven replied.

"I guess we can give Hunter a chance," Tyler said as we just walked around the mall area knowing we had to be back there shortly anyways.

"I'm still trying to figure how they keep finding out where we are?" I said.

Tyler flips open the phone that we found in the van we stole from Curtis and Vince. "I wonder if this is our problem." Tyler said as he stared at the phone.

"Where did you get that?" Steven asked as he grabbed the phone away from Tyler.

"I found it in the center console of a van we stole from 2 guys named Vince and Curtis." Tyler explained.

Steven then thinks and a start putting 2 and 2 together then says, "I bet they are tracking you on this cell phone."

"Curtis and Vince didn't look like vampires though." I said.

Tyler piped in," duh Liz they could be working for them though."

"Don't treat me like I am stupid," I hissed at Tyler.

"I was kidding honey," Tyler said as held me hand and kissed my cheek.

Steven then chucks the phone onto the ground and it breaks into a million pieces.

We take off and make it to the mall and scope the area for a broken down shack eventually finding it we saw two black figures standing still. As we got closer we could smell that they were vampires and we knew they were waiting for us, I walked towards them the one guy grabbed my shoulder to stop me.

"Are you three here to meet Hunter?" The guy dressed in black wearing a black ski mask asked us as he held onto my shoulder.

"Yes we are, and you can let go of my shoulder now!" I said as I tried to break free.

"Sorry, come with us," the man said as he let me go. "Why is it that men insist on grabbing me so hard they give me bruises?" I asked hoping to get an answer from one of the guys I was with.

"Well, dear, we wouldn't want you to try anything stupid," The other guy that was wearing the same thing too but was shorter than the other guy replied laughing.

"Ha funny," I replied rubbing my arm. For some reason their voices sounded familiar to me.

The men lead us to a nice looking house not too far from the mall. It was an older house, but well kept. The yard had a grungy rusted out truck the window was smashed out if it the truck was a tan color it was just parked there the tires were completely flat on it. You had to climb stairs in order to get to the front door. I inspected the yard I wasn't really looking for anything in particular just curious as to what my surrounding were, as we walked up the stairs. Before we knocked the door opened and a tall well-built, brown eyes and black hair man met us at the door.

"Hunter!" said Steven, hugging him.

"Nice to see you again, who are these two?" Hunter asked Steven as he winked at me.

"This is Tyler, and the girl is Liz," explained Steven.

"Nice to meet you two," Hunter shook our hands.

For once, a vampire that didn't seem to rape me with his eyes I found it kind of flattering the first couple times but it seemed every vampire I ran into seemed to want to sleep with me. I looked up his 6 foot 250 frame, his dirty blonde hair was short but styled nicely his baby blue eyes looked at me I noticed his to have a cute soul patch I was always a sucker for those.

"Follow me," Hunter said and led us into his living room, we sat down on the black leather couch I looked around his living room the walls were painted white, the rug was white his coffee table was made out of glass, the room smelt sweet I noticed some incense burning .

"Did you want anything to drink?" Hunter asked us as I heard the front door open.

"Wine," All three of us replied at the same time. I can't believe I said wine, that stuff is gross.

"Okay," Hunter replied and poured all of us a glass of wine from a large crystal glass decanter. "So what is it I can do for you three today?" Hunter asked us taking a sip of his wine.

"Do you know a vampire named Damien?" Steven asked Hunter.

"Yeah, Damien is a good friend of mine. Why do you ask?" Hunter seemed uneasy.

"Why is it that he is after Liz? And why is it he will stop at nothing to have her?" Steven asked before taking a sip of wine.

"Because he wants to get a werewolf girl pregnant, he wants to create a hybrid, a creature that is half vampire and half werewolf," Hunter explained. He looked at me and I felt uncomfortable. I choked on my wine and couldn't stop coughing. "What!" I yelled. "That is insane and disgusting!" I continued to shout as I stood up. I put my hands over my head and just paused. "I am just going to get up and walk around for a bit" I replied to Hunter as I removed my hands from my face and shot Hunter another disgusted look.

"Alright, don't be long, dear," Hunter replied as he sipped on his wine. "She sure is feisty. Damien always had something for those types. Liz doesn't stand a chance against him. He is really hard to kill. He has vampire friends all over the world and Liz will get kidnapped and become his eventually. I can keep her here for a little while and try and negotiate something with my friend," Hunter explained and then got up to make a call in another room for a short time and was back out again.

"Can we leave now?" I asked as I made my way back into the living room I was feeling uneasy.

"No I am sorry, sweetheart, you can't," Hunter replied as he nodded at the guys in the ski masks to grab me. They must have been the ones I heard coming in through the door after us.

"What is going on?" I asked as I started to panic.

"You're going to stay with me until I can negotiate something with Damien," Hunter explained and led me to another room. I told Tyler and Steven to calm down we have no other choice this has got to stop.

"What will happen to Tyler and Steven?" I asked as tears ran down my face.

"They have to leave, if Damien will negotiate anything with me he won't agree if they are here, in the mean time you can contact them anytime you want. I know it is difficult for you to trust a vampire but I might be your only hope to get Damien to leave you alone." Hunter explained to me as he wiped the tear off my cheek.

"How long do I have to stay here?" I asked Hunter.

"For a month or so as long as it takes to know it's safe to let you go," Hunter replied.

I hated that answer I didn't want my boys to leave me.

"Goodbye I will miss you guys so much" I said hugging them.

"Hey, Liz, if you need anything just call me," Tyler said and kissed me.

They left and as soon as they closed the door Hunter became violent. "I can't believe how stupid they are, leaving their precious wolf babe with me, a vampire," Hunter said, and backhanded me, sending me flying across the room. I moaned in pain and laid there.

Hunter came over to me and swept me up into his arms and threw me into one of his guards, he caught me and hung on to me tight.

"Do something with her!" Hunter hissed and stormed out of the room. The two men then took off their ski mask. I knew I knew them it was Curtis and Vince.

"What we killed you guys and your vampires how?" I asked as I was fighting to escape.

"You two left us for dead, another couple that were walking along the side of the road found us and phoned emergency from there we ended up in the hospital. Damien found us we were dying and he turned us into vampires," Curtis explained as he back handed me.

"We should have killed you when we had a chance." I snarled.

"Well you didn't you little bitch now you're going to pay for it", Vince said

I was trying to squirm my way out of his grasp but he was too strong.

"Mmm baby keep doing that don't stop," Vince said as he held me closer.

"What is she doing?" asked Curtis.

"She is grinding against me," Vince replied as he put his hands on my hips.

"What should we do with her?" asked Curtis.

"Have fun with her," Vince replied and started groping me.

"That is what I was thinking," Curtis replied as he pushed me towards the arm of the couch.

"No, go away!" I yelled and scratched Curtis in the throat.

"You little bitch!" Curtis yelled as he pushed me onto the couch. I bounced off of it and hit my head really hard on the coffee table and must have passed out.

A few hours later and I found myself on the couch. I was groggy and my head hurt.

"The little bitch is waking up," Curtis said, his hands between my leg.

"Be nice," Hunter said as he came closer.

"Hunter had his fun with you, sweetheart while you were passed out," Curtis said as he nuzzled my ear.

"Guys, cut it out," Hunter snapped as he shoved Curtis aside.

"Hunter you can't deny how cute the wolf girl is," Vince said laughing.

"I didn't deny anything. So honey I have a surprise for you." Hunter opened the door and Damien, Roman, and Jeff came walking in.

"Well, well, well, if it isn't our little wolf girl," Damien said reaching for me.

"It was really easy to get her she came right to me," Hunter replied, staring into my eyes.

I glared at him I was so pissed off I want to shift into a wolf right there.

"Hey baby, do you remember me?" Roman asked as he took me from Damien's grasp.

I just started to shake I didn't want to see him ever again and here I was being held by him.

"We will be leaving now. Thanks Hunter," Damien said as we headed out the door. Roman threw me in the van and I sat in the middle between Jeff and Roman.

"Hey, Jeff, did you have fun with her?" Roman asked as he licked the side of my face.

"No, not yet, but I will," Jeff replied, leering at me.

"I did and she is just fine," Roman said as he fondled my breasts.

I didn't know what to do anymore, would I have to live with them for the rest of my life? How would Steven and Tyler ever find me? Those were the questions I kept asking myself over and over again. I finally just realized that I was stuck with these dread full vampires so I better get used to it.

"Jeff you look really hot," I blurted out not thinking of what I just said.

Jeff just looked at me, and he smiled. "Really now?" and started rubbing my inner thigh with his hand.

We stopped at a low budget hotel just outside Lloyd and checked into a room. I followed the boys out and Damien held on to my wrist and pulled me into the hotel room. The hotel smelled like moth balls, and mold. I covered my nose and tried opening the window.

"It fucking reeks in here, do we have to stay here?" I asked in disgust. I continued to scope the room. The walls where filled with cracks and the bed was really low to the floor. The rug was a brown color and the television was small with rabbit ears.

"Yes Liz, quit complaining and put this on honey," Damien threw a night gown at me. It was transparent but I did as I was told. "Wow, honey come sit over here," Damien ordered me and patted down on the bed where he wanted me to sit. I decided to start listening instead of putting up a fight. I sat down beside them, my hair flowing down my back. I had goose bumps and I felt that it was freezing in the hotel room, so cold that I was shivering.

"Damien, why do you have a women's night gown?" I asked as I looked at him strangely.

"I picked it up after I knew where you were hiding," Damien replied smiling, "and boy do you ever look sexy in it." Damien said as he moved a bit closer to me.

" I knew that being at Hunter's was a bad mistake," I muttered.

"No, it was a good mistake," Damien laughed. "Roman did you want to come with me to grab some booze?" Damien asked.

"Sure." Roman replied.

Roman got up from the bed. Damien and Roman left the hotel leaving me and Jeff alone. I looked at Jeff and he looked at me, he got up and moved closer to me. I straddled him and began kissing him and his hands were busy on my hips. But he turned rough, he forced me on the bed and got on top of me. With one hand across my neck he stopped me from moving and with the other he pulled down his pants and he penetrated me The more I moaned the more it seemed to turn Jeff on. After he was done he got up and pulled up his pants. Shortly after, Damien and Roman returned and put the booze on the table.

"Did you want one, dear?" Damien asked me as he opened the box.

"Sure," I replied, taking one from him.

"So what did you two do while we were gone?" Roman asked Jeff.

"We had some fun," said Jeff.

They looked at me it made me feel uncomfortable.

"What?" I asked them drinking my drink. I don't know why but I actually was starting to like them as crazy as that sounds. I started to feel that I was fitting in with these vampires, but I didn't understand why.

"Nothing," Damien answered me and they came and sat down on the bed.

"This is going to sound crazy, but I am starting to like you guys," I said as I finished my drink.

"That is good," Damien replied as he moved closer to me.

God Liz what are you doing, you're supposed to hate these vampires, not fuck them, I was disgusted with myself. I kept telling myself to keep listening to them and they would eventually start to trust me. That's when I could make a move. "Care for another drink Liz?" Jeff asked as he got up to get another.

"Yeah," I replied. Jeff passed me another and sat beside me.

"So Damien what are we going to do with her?" Roman asked as he took another sip of his beer.

"I want her to have a hybrid baby," Damien replied and ran his fingers up my body.

"When do you plan on doing that?" Roman asked.

"I have to wait for the next full moon that is when she will be ready."

"What is so important about these hybrids?" Roman asked.

"Hybrids are half vampire and half werewolf" Damien replied as he shot Roman a funny look.

"Oh, okay. So in other words they will be stronger than either a vampire or a werewolf?" Roman asked between sips of beer.

"Yes, that is correct," Damien answered and caressed me so hard startled me.

I wake up with Damien's arm wrapped around in a bed in the one of the rooms.

"Damien wake up, I need out," I hissed at him, all he did was groan and held me tighter. I finally got annoyed and scratched him.

"Ouch! Liz what the fuck!" Damien shouted as he moved away.

"I need to go outside for a bit I can't sleep I am going to see if some fresh air will help me," I replied as I crawled out of bed went outside. I walked around for a bit the weather was beautiful hardly any wind just a light breeze, I took a deep breath in and I could smell the pine coming from the tress that surrounded our hotel the air was so fresh. I sat down on the step and closed my eyes for bit I started yawning so I stood back up and opened the door back to the room, I came out and crawled back into bed I still didn't feel tired I nudged Damien to see if he was still awake. "Damien, are you awake?" I asked.

"Yes you woke me up the first time I just waited for you to come back inside," Damien replied.

"Damien, why is Hunter so aggressive?" I asked.

"He likes to be the dominant one," Damien replied and put his arm around me again.

"I thought you were the dominant one?" I asked looking confused.

"Yeah, I guess we both try to be. Hunter he is different he doesn't like to let girls in his life," Damien explained. "He does like you but you will notice when you hang out with him he will try and be tough on the outside but on the inside he is a softy," Damien said.

"How do you know he likes me?" I asked as I played with my hair.

"He told me on the phone when he called to tell me you were at his house. He said you were attractive, and cute," Damien admitted.

"Oh! What is it with you and all the other guys always wanting me?" I asked and turned to face him.

"Because it is a vampire's fantasy to be with a female werewolf," Damien replied as he kissed me on the cheek.

"Is a female werewolf hard to come by?" I asked Damien as I closed my eyes.

"Yes, that is why I didn't want to lose you," Damien replied as we both eventually fell asleep.

I woke up to the sun in my face covering my face with my hand I slowly opened my eyes and got out of bed. I was still groggy and half asleep I noticed the boys were sitting on the end of the other bed.

"Good morning Liz," Roman said to me as he grabbed my ass and laughed, I turned around and glared at him.

"Don't, I am bitchy in the morning," I snarled as I went into the bathroom.

"She sure is feisty, I love her attitude," Roman said laughing.

"I know, she is quite a girl," Damien replied as he poured himself a cup of coffee.

I got out of the shower and stepped out of the bathroom with just a bath towel wrapped around me. Damien was standing there holding onto the nightgown..

"Excuse me please, I am not wearing that all day," I said to Damien.

"Awwweee," Damien replied as he sulked a bit.

I grabbed my old clothing, and stood up right when I was about to take a step forward Damien grabbed the towel and pulled it down.

"Hey!" I yelled at Damien, and ran back into the washroom I was so embarrassed.

"That was funny," Roman said laughing.

I got ready and walked out of the washroom and tried to ignore them, but it was very hard to do so.

"Hey, honey, that was a nice view," Damien said winking at me.

"Shut up," I said hitting him.

"What, honey? I am telling you the truth and that was for not going with my idea" Damien laughed.

"You didn't have to do that to let me know what you thought," I said glaring at him.

"It was joke, Liz, now let's get going. We are running out of time." We loaded all the bags in the vehicle.

"So where are we going?" I asked Damien as I hopped in the front seat.

"We are going to were the other head vampire in Winnipeg." Damien answered as he dug around in his pocket and pulled out his phone to get his GPS ready.

Great, I thought. How well is this going to pan out? I was in for a long car ride. We drove for a couple of hours then we stopped and got out to stretch and to eat. This time we didn't even stop to stay in a hotel room we keep on driving and finally made it driving threw Winnipeg and about 15 minutes out of the city we turned left on a long gravel road, then passing a pond with ducks swimming about finally making to our destination. We parked in a garage of some old looking dump. The house looked like it was 100 years old. The wind was howling and the screen door kept flying open. I looked around the yard and noticed a pond in the yard in the middle of the pond there was a huge cement goldfish statue with water spraying out of its mouth. Just as I was about to take a closer look a short scruffy looking vampire greeted us at the entrance and welcomed us in.

"Conrad will be right with you," the scruffy vampire said as he continued to sweep the hallway.

"Damien is that you?" called a voice the living room. "Come on in, don't be shy my friend," the voice demanded.

We all took off our shoes and went into the living and sat down on the couch.

"Conrad, this is Liz, the werewolf," Damien said as he introduced me to Conrad.

"Ah she is beautiful little thing isn't she?" Conrad replied as he studied me. I was feeling a bit uncomfortable. "So what brings you here?" Conrad asked as he took a sip of his wine.

"We needed a place to stay for a couple of days," Damien replied.

"Yeah sure, how rude of me did you guys want anything to drink?" Conrad asked.

"Yes, we will have a glass of wine," Damien answered for all of us.

A slim tall lady vampire poured us all a glass of wine and handed each of us a glass. I wasn't a big fan of wine but I didn't want to be rude so I sipped on it.

"So, Liz, you are a werewolf, did you know it's a full moon tonight?" Conrad asked me as he looked at his watch.

Shit! I actually had no idea but I didn't want them to know that so I just nodded. I really needed to escape now, and I knew what Damien's plans were and I was not interested in his plans at all.

"How long are we staying here for?" I asked Damien as I swirled the rest of wine around in my glass.

"For a few days," Damien said and sat down beside me.

"I have a bed for you two upstairs whenever the wolf girl is ready," Conrad said and finished the rest of his wine.

I felt my stomach turn when he said that, all I knew is that I didn't want to get pregnant with Damien's kid. That would be disgusting and I was so scared I wanted Tyler and Steven back so bad.

"I am ready when you are, love," Damien said with a knowing smile. Yuck I could tell he could barely wait, he has been waiting for this moment for a long time now. I looked up at the clock and it was almost 10:00 pm. I would change into a wolf at midnight. I started to feel sick and light headed I stood up and everything spun. I stood there holding my head I dropped to the floor in pain.

"Damien you better hurry it is beginning she will be a wolf at the stroke of midnight," Conrad helped me stand me up and pushed me at Damien who caught me and carried me upstairs. I finally came to my senses when I was lying on a bed and I knew what was happening.

"No, Damien not yet," I said pushing him off me. He was getting angry.

"Now is the best time, love don't fight me and you won't get hurt," Damien hissed as and kissed me forcefully. I let him do all the work. It felt good and I started moaning.

"Mmm, Liz, your eyes turned red," Damien was breathing heavier now, his thrusting more urgent.

He was biting my neck, and I dug my nails into his back. I could tell he was about to come. He went faster and deeper then stopped with a groan. He lay still for a few seconds. He pulled out and rolled off me and held me close.

"Liz, that felt good," Damien said, still panting.

"It is midnight," Damien replied and I shot out of bed and pulled on my clothes. He got dressed and followed me downstairs where the other vampires were still awake talking in the living room.

I could feel myself starting to shift and I had no control over it so I just let it happen. I could hear Conrad yelling at Damien.

"Shit, Damien we were supposed to lock her away before she had a chance to shift!" I growled and my fur around my neck lifted up I was a very pissed off bitch right now. I leaped at Jeff and I was on him trying to bite him but he threw me off and I hit the wall. I was back on four legs and growled when all of a sudden Conrad shot me with something. I felt myself shift back into a human I was all curled up in a ball, freezing.

"I will get a blanket," Conrad said as he left to find one.

"What happened, why did she change back?" Roman asked, confused.

"I shot her with a serum which calms the wolf effect" said Conrad as he opened the blanket.

"Liz, are you okay?" Damien asked, turning me over.

"I am tired," I replied closing me eyes.

"Okay, we will let you sleep," Damien replied as he picked me up and brought me up the room and lay me on the bed.

The next morning I found myself full of energy, I ran downstairs and where I could smell fresh brewed coffee. As I searched the cupboards for a coffee cups I felt someone behind me and the hairs on the back of my neck stood up. I quickly turned and Conrad was there.

"You scared me," I said, almost dropping a cup.

"Sorry, how are you feeling?" Conrad stepped closer.

"Great," I answered as I poured myself a cup of coffee.

"I see why the boys fancy you so much, dear," Conrad put his hands around my waist hips and started to smell my hair.

I didn't move. "It is because I am the only female werewolf you guys have ever found," I replied as I moved away. I took my coffee into the living room and Damien followed me and sat down next to me.

"How are you feeling?" Damien asked and put his hand on my leg.

"Good," I replied and sipped on my coffee.

"That is good to hear," Damien said as he got up to get a cup of coffee.

I could overhear Damien and Conrad talking in the kitchen.

"How long is she here for?" Conrad asked Damien.

"However long I am here for," Damien replied.

"Why are you taking her everywhere, she is a wolf, vampires and wolves hate each other. You actually don't care about her do you?" Conrad asked Damien.

"No, I just needed to get her pregnant, I could care less about her," Damien replied.

"What if she doesn't get pregnant? Are you going to keep wasting your time?" Conrad asked as he looked over and spotted me standing there.

"If you fucks don't care about me then let me go back to my family!" I yelled and threw the coffee cup at them, it splashed everywhere. I ran upstairs and fell onto the bed and started to cry.

"Liz, I am sorry," Damien said as he slowly sat down beside me.

"Go away," I said and turned to ignore him.

"I didn't mean what I said. It's Conrad. He doesn't like wolves," he explained.

"He sure was trying to get close to me," I replied between sniffles.

"Yeah that is because you're a female, he will do that".

"Isn't that why you like me too?" I asked.

"It was at first, but you grew on me," I smiled, but then I felt queasy I ran to the bathroom, I sat there by the toilet, I must have been the bathroom for a long time because when I stepped out all the guys where there waiting for me. I looked at them and went into the living room. Something else was happening to me I just couldn't figure it out.

Chapter Six

THE HYBRID

I grab Jeff's cup and start chugging it down like water.

"Are you alright, Liz?" Jeff asked.

"I don't know," I replied. I looked over at Jeff but he just stood there, looking back at me with a strange expression on his face.

"Damien I need to talk to you," Conrad said as they both went outside.

"I am going to go with them," Roman said as he stepped outside too.

The three of them start talking outside. Roman piped up, " Did you see her drink the whole cup of blood like nothing?".

"Yes we did that's why we came out here to talk Roman," they both said.

"She is starting to get cravings for blood," Conrad said

"That can only mean one thing, she is a hybrid already we just didn't know it," Damien replied.

"We have to watch out for the color of her eyes," Conrad said.

They all looked each other and started smiling.

Meanwhile inside the house I looked at Jeff, I ran to him and threw him on the couch I get on him and started kissing him. I was grinding against him, he sure wasn't complaining.

"Mmm, Liz, what is happening to you?' Jeff asked as he was kissing my neck.

"I don't know, shut up and fuck me," I hissed at him as I tore apart his black t-shirt he had on. Jeff fumbled trying to take off his pants scared the others might walk in on them. Jeff finally gets them off meanwhile I been naked for what felt like 12 hours already. He started kissing me all over while his hands rubbed everywhere else. "Hurry up and fuck me," I screamed.

In the midst of having sex Jeff noticed my eyes going red, he just stared at me.

"What is wrong?" I asked Jeff as he started slowing down.

"Your eyes have turned red," Jeff said, .

"So?" I replied.

"Nothing, it was just kind of strange, it just caught me off guard, " Jeff replied as he sped up again.

The door swings open and the three guys walk in and see what's going on.

Damien shouts, "Can I join?"

Jeff looks over and sees the three of them standing there looking at him laughing at him.

"I see you couldn't help but tap the sweet ass either," Roman smirked.

I push Jeff off and run to the closest bedroom damn that's so embarrassing.

Conrad and Roman leave the living room to go upstairs to look for a certain book Conrad had about hybrids. Damien stood there still laughing at Jeff and poking fun at him.

"Stop laughing your just jealous," Jeff muttered as he wiped some sweat off his forehead.

"Not really I wouldn't want to be caught," Damien replied. "Anyways I am going to go talk to Liz," Damien said as he started walking away.

"Wait I want to tell you something," Jeff replied as he gets up and puts his pants back on then walks over to Damien and tells him about Liz's eyes turning a red color which freaked him out. Damien comes into the room which I ran into. I'm lying on the bed all naked and sweaty as he rolls me on my back and looks over me and studies me closely.

"Leave me alone," I said as I muffled into the pillow.

"Awww sweet heart I got something important to tell, you are a hybrid I can smell vampire mixed in with werewolf," Damien explained.

"How is that possible, you guys did something didn't you? As if it wasn't tough enough being a werewolf you guys had to make me into a vampire," I snarled as I sat up and moved away from Damien I pulled the blanket out from underneath us and wrapped myself in it.

"No we had nothing to do with this dear. I am thinking your parents were both werewolf and vampire," Damien replied as he scooted closer to me.

"Why did I just notice it now?" I asked as I turned my head to look at him.

"If I were to take a guess it was because you have been around vampires for a long time and that part of you kicked in, otherwise I am not too sure," Damien explained.

"Great now I need to cope with that," I replied.

"This is interesting actually truly amazing! I have never seen a hybrid before," Damien said with excitement.

"Well I am glad you find this so amazing because I don't," I pouted as I stood up I was about to go step out of the bedroom when he spoke up again.

"If anyone finds out about you won't be safe," Damien adds in

"I was never safe to begin with though. And what do you know about hybrids?" I asked.

"We don't really know anything about hybrids. All we know is that if you are half and half you are very powerful," Damien replied as he stared intently at me.

"I'm scared," I replied.

"I know you are Liz, but I will protect you," Damien replied.

We walk back out into the living room where everyone else, Jeff tosses me my clothes and I put them on, Damien waits for the others to come back downstairs. Conrad and Roman finally come downstairs meeting up with Damien in the living room. Damien tells the other the new situation that has arisen.

"Jeff, do you want to go for a walk?" I ask

"I would be delighted to escort you my dear." Jeff laughs

"No more hanky panky," Roman yells as the door slams

Jeff and I go down this nice rocky trail down to the pond.

Jeff starts kissing my neck and whispers in my ear. "Now we can finish where we left off I see your plan Liz."

"Well you are half undressed," I laughed.

"By the way you owe me for a new shirt," Jeff grinned

"How about you just shut up and fuck me". I said getting in patient.

Jeff just laughed as laid me down on the grass, gently pulling my pants down and pulling down his he then inserts himself inside me.

Meanwhile, Damien and Roman sit down on the couch and Conrad walks over with a green leather book. "If she finds out how much power she has she will be stronger than any of us," Conrad explained as he puts the green leather book on the coffee table. Conrad then flipped the book open the pages were filled with pictures of huge werewolves and vampires.

"I really don't know what I am looking for, but I will read this book and see what useful information I can find," Conrad suggested as he skimmed through the pages.

"That sounds good," Roman replied.

Jeff and I come from our jaunt in the woods and Jeff goes into the living and I go to the bathroom to have myself a bath.

"How was your walk?" Roman asked.

"It was nice," Jeff replied as he sat down next to Damien.

Conrad noticed me as he walked past and just walked right into the bathroom with me.

"Hey Liz I forgot to tell you something," Conrad said and he stopped in his tracks and watched me undress and as I bent over and turned on the taps. I then felt someone watching me.

"Conrad you scared me, I am sorry what did you need?" I asked as I felt embarrassed. and tried to cover myself up.

"I forget, you can keep undressing though," Conrad said as he came closer to me.

Conrad grabbed me by my hips and pushed himself into me.

"Liz, I want you so bad," Conrad said as he gently kissed my cheek.

I smirked and walked away from leaving him in the bathroom I go over to the dresser that was in the bedroom. Conrad followed me and put his hands on my hips I turned around to face him.

"I know you want me. So what do the guys think of me now?" I asked .

"They want you even more," Conrad replied as he stared at me.

"How bad do you want me?" I asked Conrad. As I pushed him toward the bathroom he looked shock and kept back peddling until the counter stopped him I then pushed him on the bathroom counter, and stood in front of him.

"Really bad, babe," he replied and slid off the counter and grabbed me tightly and pulled me in and started nibbling on my ear. His mouth then came around and gave me a nice long kiss it felt so good.

I then grabbed him and lifted off his shirt and started running my lips down his chest until I got to the button on his jeans

"Have you ever been with a wolf girl?" I asked as I looked up at him with my sexy blue eyes and undid he pants and pulled them down.

"No," Conrad replied as he closed his eyes and groaned and stepped out of his pants and then he grabbed my hand and led me out of the bathroom and t led me to the bedroom where he picked me up and laid me down on the bed, knelt beside me and then hovered over me. He stared into my blue eyes and kissed my lips gently. All of a sudden there was a commotion downstairs and Damien shouted, " Conrad, Liz where the hell are you?" Conrad and I run into the bathroom and quickly got ourselves dressed then run back into the bedroom and sit on the bed.

"We're in the bedroom on the right Damien," Conrad yells

"Conrad, hurry! Get the fuck downstairs now!" Damien yelled in a panic.

This was not the kind of interruption that Conrad wanted. He got up reluctantly and went running downstairs. As he looked around he saw there was blood everywhere.

"What the hell is going on?" Conrad yelled.

I was still sitting on the bed wondering what all the commotion was about so I got up and peeked out the door and seen someone running down the hallway., .

"Liz are you up here?" I heard someone yell it sounded like Tyler's voice.

"Yea I'm in the bedroom on the right," as Tyler comes storming into the bedroom.

"What are you doing here?" I asked him, wondering why he couldn't just smell and had to ask where I was.

"I am here to save you, honey," Tyler replied. "Follow me and hurry Steven is outside making sure we have an escape route, I'll explain everything on the way." Tyler said.

"Tyler, you are going to get killed," I said as we ran downstairs. We were about to run out the door when Damien and Conrad blocked our way out.

"And what do you think you are doing with our girl?" Damien threateningly asked

"I am taking her. She is mine," Tyler hissed.

Just before Conrad and Damien could make any moves, Steven knocked Damien them over the head with a shovel. Conrad looked over and seen Steven as Tyler and I ran and pushed him down.

"Come on, let's go. We are running out of time!" Steven yelled as the three of us ran out the door and down the driveway to the truck that Steven and Tyler brought. I looked back and seen Conrad getting up and starting to chase after us.

We got into the truck and drove off, I looked back and seen Conrad standing in the middle of the street just staring at us as we drove away you could tell he was severely pissed off.

"Liz, are you okay?" Tyler asked as he put his hand on my lap.

"No, not really," I replied. I looked out of the window at all the dead trees in the ditch by the highway and I started to cry.

"Well, do you want to talk about it?" Tyler asked.

"No not right now. Maybe later, when I am ready, I just need some time to myself," I replied as I wiped the tears off my face.

"Okay, I understand," Tyler said. I could feel him just staring at me. "Why are you staring at me?" I asked looking at him.

"I missed you so much. When I found out they came and took you it felt like an eternity to finally find out where they were hiding you," Tyler explain as his eyes watered up.

"Aw, you really did miss me? I thought that you had given up on finding me," I reassured him and moved closer to him.

As the kilometers clicked by I eventually fell asleep, my head resting on Tyler's shoulder. I woke up with a fright. But it was only Tyler snoring and there was no way I was falling back asleep with the noise Tyler was making. I sat up and rubbed my eyes. I was still strangely tired.

"How did you sleep?" Steven asked me.

"Good until Tyler started snoring," I replied laughing.

"Yeah. Tyler hasn't slept for days. He was really worried about you," Steven explained as we pulled into a gas station. "I need to top up the tank I want a full tank for the long trip to Prince Albert." Steven said as he unbuckled his seat belt.

Steven got out of the truck and filled the tank then he went inside to pay. I sat there waiting for Tyler to wake up, but he didn't. Steven got into the truck and we drove off again. As we turned back onto the highway he tossed me a bag of chips. "Here, I thought you might be hungry." I told him I felt as if I spend my days inside vehicles.

"Steven, how did you and Tyler find out where I was?" I asked "We went back to Hunter's place and I held Curtis down and held a knife to his throat while Tyler made sure no one came around. He squealed like a little pig and told me everything." Steven explained as he turned on some funky jazz music.

"What this that crap your listen to?" I asked.

"Fine you find something better." Steven responded.

"Oh, anyways I have something I need to tell you, Tyler. I am so scared I don't know what to think. I have no idea what is going on or what any of it means, but..." I said as I turned the station and found something better to listen to I then looked out the window and drifted into silence. As the song on the radio ended Steven said, "Well you can talk about it when you are ready."

I just stared out the window watching the world go by I seen a couple of deer eating grass on the side of the road a moose hiding in the bush. I saw Steven almost run over a gopher, stupid animals. I finally thought about it and couldn't.

"Yesterday I found out that I was actually a hybrid. I don't know how or why," I said "I'm still trying to figure out how it happened and why me." I explained I looked over at Steven.

"Are you sure?" Steven asked me as he looked at me, "You smell different but I figured that was because you were around those awful vampires for such a long time." Steven answered as he tried to look at me but he knew he had to focus on the highway.

"But there's more. I saw one of the other vampires were drinking blood and I'm not sure I want to tell you what happened next," I replied as I turned back on looked out the window.

"Liz don't leave me hanging like that" Steven replied.

"Fine I will tell you. So I grabbed it from him and drank all of it, I don't know why but I did I realise now that I have been feeling really weird ever since," I explained. I couldn't look at him, so all the time I kept staring out the window. Steven just sat there in shock he didn't know what to say. I had so much on mind, like why couldn't I have a normal life, why did I have to run all the time, what is going to happen?

After a long drive we finally made it to another hotel where I threw myself onto the bed. I lay staring at the ceiling and Tyler came to lie next to me.

"Before this all happened I was getting ready to have a bath and I still never got a bath, so therefore I am taking a bath right now," I said as I went into the washroom.

I poured the bath and lay in the nice warm water just soaking in all the thoughts running through my mind. Liz get it together I am stronger than this, I mean I have to be now, everything will be ok.

Meanwhile back at the vampire's house

"For fucks sakes, how did we let this happen?" Damien shouted as he picked up a chair and threw across the room at Jeff.

"Calm down, Damien," Conrad said and pinned Damien against the wall so he would stop this nonsense.

"We finally had her, and now she is a hybrid and we lost her again," Damien replied and paced back and forth, agitated.

"I know, we have to get rid of those boys," Conrad said as he was trying to think of a plan.

"I will get my friends to help us out again," Damien said and whipped out his phone.

"I wonder if there are any other females out there, I mean she can't be the only one," Jeff said, butting in to their conversation.

"Probably, Jeff, but we don't know where," Damien was annoyed.

Conrad and Jeff sat there in silence as Damien spoke on the phone.

"Yeah, can you guys keep an eye out for a young female werewolf? She will be with two male werewolves. Catch them and kill the boys, but keep the girl alive," Damien ordered as he flipped the phone shut.

"I wonder if she went back home," mused Jeff.

"Why would she do that? There is nothing there for her." Damien answered and rolled his eyes.

"I don't know. It was a suggestion," Jeff glared at Damien.

"Why would she even go with them? That is what I can't figure out," said Conrad as he got himself a drink.

"Because she loves that Tyler, I am going outside I need fresh air I need to cool off," Damien replied and walked outside.

"Conrad, I think Damien has feelings for her," suggested Jeff.

"I know he does," Conrad agreed.

"Did he tell you that he did?" Jeff asked and turned on the fire in the fireplace.

"Not exactly, but I can tell by the way he acts when he is around her and now that she is gone, he is pissed off," Conrad explained and sat down on the couch.

Damien came back inside the house and he just stood there with a blank look on his face.

"I am going to go pick up Hunter and find her," Damien said as he got out his phone.

"What, you don't even know where she is," Conrad said as he stood up and walked towards Damien.

"I don't care, I am going to go look for her," Damien scowled and left the house.

"He is insane, we better go with him," Conrad said as he looked at Jeff.

"Okay," Jeff replied as he got up.

Meanwhile I got out of the bath and dried myself off and stared at the mirror I need to find some clothes I thought to myself.

"Guys, I want to go home and start living a normal life," I said as I crawled under the covers.

"Liz, you know that is impossible," Tyler said as he got under the covers with me.

"I want to start acting as if my life is normal again. I want to dance, do some photography and art," I said.

"Well we will start some of that stuff, especially with such a nice view under these covers," Tyler joked as he kissed my forehead.

The next morning I woke up and we had an early start to our day back on the road again, I said, "Can we go and get me some clothes instead of being in this housecoat all day?"

"You can do without," both boys said.

"Men!" I shouted.

We soon stopped at a department store Tyler ran in leaving Steven in the truck with me.

"How are you holding up?" Steven asked.

"I am alright I guess," I answered as I watched for Tyler.

I saw Tyler run out of the department store with a couple bags. He flung the truck door open and tossed me the bags. I opened the bags and rummaged through the clothing I held them up to get a better look, I was actually impressed he bought me a black skirt with flowers going up the side and a purple tank top.

I slipped the clothing on my cold body in the truck. Steven started the truck up and off we went. We turned on to the highway and I watched the endless rows of tress pass us. The sun was shining but it was windy out it still seemed too early for me, but I knew we needed to get on the road as soon as possible.

"Thanks for the clothing," I said.

"You're welcome," Tyler answered.

"Where are we going this time?' I asked.

"It is a surprise," Steven said and smiled.

After a few hours of driving we arrived in Prince Albert. The streets were familiar but I was confused. then it hit me we were in my home town.

"You took me to my home town!" I shouted as I kissed Steven on the cheek.

"Where do you live?" Steven asked me as he laughed.

"Just keep going and I will tell you."

We made it to my place and I had almost forgotten what it looked like, I had not been home for a few months.

"Liz, we can stay here in PA for a little while, but not for long," Tyler said but I didn't care, I was so happy to be home I hugged them both.

I phoned Daniel and invited him over for a few drinks. The doorbell rang, there he was.

"Hey Liz, where have you been?" Daniel asked as he hugged me.

"Oh around, I took a road trip," I replied lying through my teeth.

"Oh, okay I was getting worried," Daniel replied, not convinced.

"This is my boyfriend, Tyler, and that's my friend Steven."

"Nice to meet you," Daniel said and shook their hands.

I was finally home. I felt so happy being back with my friends and inside my home instead of hotels or inside vampire's homes. I sat there not saying a word when all of a sudden a hand waved in front of me.

"Liz, are you okay?" Daniel asked me as he came closer to me.

"Um, yeah," I replied snapping out of my daze.

"Liz, can I talk to you in private please?" signaled for me to come with him outside.

"Yeah, sure." I followed him outside.

Daniel was leaning up against my house and after silence he asked, "So, was I right about you being a lycanthrope?"

"Yeah, you were right, but I am a hybrid," I told him and stared down at the ground staring at the rocks that surrounded my step.

"Really, so being a hybrid means one of your parents is a werewolf and the other one is a vampire. Wow, this is exciting! So what is it really like?" Daniel asked as excitement filled his eyes.

"It isn't all rosy. I crave blood I want to tear everything apart, I am always running away and I can never stay in one place. I mean it is kind of cool because I can jump high, and my speed and agility is amazing and my hearing and my eyesight are both so detailed I can see for miles and hear a single pin drop. I can also shift into a werewolf at any time. So I guess it does have some good sides.," I explained.

"That is hot, I am sorry, I love werewolves and vampires but I never dreamt of meeting one." After pause he continued, "Can you make me one?"

"No, besides Tyler and Steven would be upset with me. And even if I wanted to I don't know how," I told him, annoyed at his question.

"What do Tyler and Steven have to do with my decision? I know how you would change me," Daniel replied. He was begging me.

"No I won't, Daniel. It is dangerous. Tyler and Steven are werewolves like me. Now if you will excuse me I am going back inside."

"Fine, but I hope you change your mind." Daniel followed me inside.

"What where you two chatting about?" Steven asked as he stood up.

"Nothing much Daniel was just asking how I was doing and how my road trip was," I replied.

"I see, anyways I need to go for a walk stretch my legs after a long drive," Steven said as he headed outside.

I followed Steven outside, I wanted to ask him how a werewolf would infect a human. I was curious to see if it was even possible.

"Steven, are you okay?" I asked as I looked up at the sky I loved staring at the stars they were so relaxing.

"Yeah, I just find it hot in your house and I needed to stretch," Steven replied.

"I was wondering if it is possible to change human into a werewolf," I asked.

"Yes, you can infect a human by getting your blood in an open wound. Or though unprotected sex. I know Daniel would love that. I also heard that if you even scratch a human that could infect them too. Why?" he asked as he looked at me strangely.

"Daniel wants me to change him and I told him no," I explained. "Good, you told him no. He doesn't think about the downsides to being a werewolf, he is just thinking about the cool things we can do. If he ever does find a werewolf who agrees to change him he will soon realize the mistake he has made. Most werewolves after they infect a human will leave that person by themselves until they can prove themselves worthy of being in the pack," Steven explained and walked towards a tree in my back yard.

"I don't think Daniel realizes that. What is over there that has caught your interest?" I asked.

"This plant, if used correctly it can knock a vampire out for a few hours. I believe it is called Poison Chive," ripped a chunk off and showed it to me. I backed away from it the smell was sweet and it was a purple color the leaves were soft looking.

"I can't touch it," I said backing away.

"I know, I wasn't going to let you touch it," Steven threw the plant back on the ground and headed back inside and I followed.

"Hey, Daniel, sorry I was outside I wanted to ask Steven something," I explained as I joined Daniel and Tyler who were hanging out.

"It's okay, Tyler and I were talking up a storm," Daniel replied and stood up. "Well I am on my way," Damien said and prepared to leave.

"Okay, thanks for coming over," I hugged him and he left. "Oh okay, well I will show you guys around this place," I said as and led them upstairs.

"We all have to sleep on this bed?" Steven said raising his eyebrows at me.

"Yeah unfortunately I don't have a bigger bed, unless you want to sleep on the couch," I replied.

"Yeah, I think I will, that way you can have time with Tyler," Steven replied and went downstairs to get changed.

Tyler came up to me and started undressing me. He slid my purple tank top over my head and kissed me at the same time, he undid the zipper on my skirt I stepped out of skirt now only in my underwear. Tyler lifted me up and sat me on top of my dresser his hands wondered my body. I put my arms around his neck and kissed his lips I lifted his shirt over his head. I stopped suddenly and looked away staring at my white wall in my room.

"Hey baby what is wrong?" Tyler asked.

"There is something I need to tell you, and I don't know how you are going to react," I replied still not looking at him I couldn't bare to tell him what monster I was but I knew I needed to.

"Try me," said Tyler.

"Well when I was with the vampires I found out something about me, I am not only a werewolf but I am also a vampire," I explained to Tyler still too scared and embarrassed to look at him.

"Oh." Tyler backed away from me.

"You think I am gross now, don't you?" I asked and looked at him, waiting.

"No I don't but I need some time to think about being with you still." Tyler got up from my bed.

"You don't want to be with me anymore?" I asked as I started to cry some more.

"I don't know what I want," Tyler replied and closed the door behind him.

I was so upset I went running downstairs and ran out of my house, I kept running and running. I was never good at controlling my emotions being by myself seemed to help most of the time.

"What the hell Tyler, why is Liz so upset?" Steven asked Tyler.

"I told her I didn't know if I wanted to be with her anymore." Tyler replied.

"Why?" Steven asked with great disgust in his voice.

"Because of what she is," Tyler tried to explain to Steven.

"You're an asshole," said Steven who then ran out the door and tried running after Liz.

I ran to a park that was a couple blocks away from my house and sat on a swing I was crying I was so upset, I was just sitting there when I heard a voice come from the bushes next to me.

"Who is there?" I asked as I got off my swing.

"Little girls shouldn't be out so late," A tall guy wearing a ski mask answered as he came out from the bush with a knife.

I was not in the mood to deal with this shit, I just looked at him.

"I am the wrong bitch to pick on tonight," I answered as I ran up to him and bit his neck. I couldn't believe I was doing this but if felt good. He screamed as I drank his blood. I threw him to the ground after I was finished. I looked at him lying there I stared at the blood that surrounded his lifeless body. What kind of a monster have I become? I should have stayed with Damien, I told myself and I walked away from the body. I walked around aimlessly. Behind me I could hear Steven calling for me but I ignored him and kept walking. I heard a vehicle behind me I turned around to see, it pulled up beside me and three men wearing hoods jumped out and surrounded me.

"You have to be kidding me, I am really bitchy tonight," I hissed as my eyes turned red and I flew at one of them.

"Hey, Liz, cut it out!" The one man said as he threw me off him. He put his hood down and the other men did the same.

"Damien," I said surprised as I jumped at him hugging him tightly.

"Yes, Liz, we came back for you. We took our chances and came to your home town," Damien explained, smiling.

"Good, because Tyler and I broke up, he couldn't stand the sight of me after I told him what I was," I replied as I started crying again.

"How can Tyler not want to be with you?" Damien asked as we stepped into the van.

"Because he hates vampires so much he can't stand that I have vampire in me," I explained. I felt ashamed.

"You can't help it, sweetie," Damien said and sat down beside me.

"I know, but anyways off topic where are we going?" I asked looking at Damien.

"Back home." Damien put his arm around me.

I didn't know if I wanted to be with anyone at this point in my life I was so confused, all I wanted was to go home and live a normal life.

I looked around at all the vampires that where in the van, I said, "hey!" to Jeff, Conrad, Roman, Hunter, , "Long time no see."

I felt uneasy that Hunter, where there as last time I was with them it ended badly. I tried not to look at them.

"So, Liz, you are a hybrid?" Hunter asked.

"Yyyyyeessssss" I answered feeling nervous around Hunter.

"Why do you look nervous?" asked James.

"Because I don't like you guys." I moved closer to Damien.

I secretly had a crush on Hunter but I didn't want him to find out though. I didn't think he liked me as he never showed that he might be attracted to me in any way. I kept staring at him although I really wanted to jump on him.

"Well, honey, you're going to have to get to like us because we are not going anywhere," Hunter replied with an evil grin. His smile made me melt inside.

"Hey, Damien, is she your new lover?" Hunter asked Damien laughing.

"Maybe. None of your business, though," Damien hissed.

"Where is Vince and Curtis?" I asked.

"They stayed back at the house, we didn't need everyone to tag along," Hunter replied.

"What are your plans with her, Damien? I mean, you can't fall in love with her?" Hunter asked looking concerned.

"Hey I am still here," I snapped glaring at Hunter.

"I know that, I am just telling Damien why it is a bad idea to get feelings for you," Hunter replied.

"You can't tell him how to feel," I snapped.

"I know but I can give him my opinion," Hunter said.

"I don't know. Why can't I fall in love with her?" Damien asked Hunter.

"Yeah Hunter why can't he fall in love with me?" I asked sarcastically.

"Because she is a werewolf too," Hunter explained.

"I know, but she is also a vampire," Damien said

"So what if I am a werewolf, I am also a vampire so I don't even know where I belong anymore," I replied.

"I am not saying you don't belong with us, all I am saying is Damien needs to be careful," Hunter said.

"Thanks for the help but I will find out for myself," Damien replied.

"Hey not to interrupt but where are we staying tonight?" Conrad asked.

"We will be staying in the nearest hotel tonight so everyone can get some rest," Hunter said.

"What about this hotel on the left of us?" Roman asked.

"Yeah sure we can't be too picky," Hunter replied.

Roman pulled into the parking lot of a motel it was decent looking at least. It wasn't busy at all and there was vines that grew up the side of the motel. At this point I didn't care were we stayed I wasn't going to get much sleep anyways. The anxiety that over flowed my body was making me sick. We stepped out of the van and walked into our room it smelled like spices and febreez not really a good mixture.

"Guys I don't have a night gown," I said as I looked around the room. The wall paper was peeling a bit, there was a green couch in the corner looked a little worn out. The room was small was the worst one I stayed at.

"Here I have something you can wear put this on," Hunter said and gave me a shirt.

I looked at the shirt in disgust, it was a muscle top with blood stains all over it.

"Yuck, it's gross." I threw it back at him.

"Liz no time to be stubborn," Hunter snarled.

"Can you at least give me one that isn't stained?" I asked, crossing my arms.

"Why what is wrong, Liz? You don't want to show off your body?" Conrad leered.

I glared at him and flipped him off.

"You're too funny, Conrad," I hissed as I got undressed in the bathroom. I looked at the mirror and I cringed it was horrible. I turned around and headed out of the bathroom and slowly made my way to the bed. I sat there everyone stared at me in silence.

"What is going on? Why are you staring at me?" I asked as I started to get panicky.

"You're not shy are you?" Damien asked.

"No not really remember the insistent with Jeff and I, the only difference is Hunter wasn't there," I explained as I started to yawn.

"Did you have to remind them?" Jeff asked.

"Sorry but it's true," I replied.

"You really are a cute girl," Damien said as he came over to me and started tickling me.

"Stop I hate it when I get tickled," I shouted as I kicked and squirmed.

"Okay leave the bitch alone," said Hunter as he stormed off outside to find something in the van.

"Wow, he really hates me doesn't' he?" I asked, shocked. Damien stopped tickling me and he stood up.

"He is upset that I care so much about you and that you're a wolf," Damien explained.

"Oh, why did he come then if he hates me so much?" I asked and sat up.

"He doesn't hate you, he is a hard character to read," Jeff replied.

Hunter came back in and was pissed off.

"What is wrong?' I asked.

"I can't find a paper and it is important," Hunter explained.

"It will show up," Damien replied.

"It better or else I will be searching all of you guys especially the wolf," Hunter stared right at me and gave me the creeps.

I was sick and tired of being abused and treated like I asked for this life so I stole Damien's jacket and put on my shoes before I left I whispered to Hunter. "I really was beginning to like you, but you pushed my buttons too many times," I then looked up at Hunter's brown eyes and I pushed him out of the way and slammed the door in his face as I left.

"Way to go, Hunter. You pissed her off." Damien came after me.

"So let her cool off," Hunter said.

"Why do you hate her so much?" Jeff asked.

"I...I don't hate her, I hate the fact that she is a wolf, I hate the fact that I care about her." Hunter sat down on the edge of the bed.

"You actually care about her?" asked Jeff.

"What the hell did I just say? Yes, and it bothers me so much that she reminds me of someone, I can't place a finger on who, though. Anyways I better go see where Damien and Liz went to I guess I should explain myself to Liz" Hunter said as he went outside to see where Damien went.

I didn't know where I was going but I needed time to think I looked up on top of the hill this hill looked familiar then it dawned on me, my friends and I played on this hill when we were kids. Then I snapped out of it and spotted a pack of wolves standing there staring at me. These wolves, there were something different about them, they weren't normal wolves. I think they could be werewolves. I took a closer look and they didn't move.

"Are you werewolves?" I asked them hoping they might answer.

I heard a voice call me, and I knew it was Damien I rolled my eyes and stood there. He will find me, I thought, and stared at these wolves.

"Liz, there you are." Damien was running up to me.

The wolves started growling and showing their teeth at him. The alpha wolf looked at me and shifted into a woman I couldn't believe it, another female wolf.

"You must me Liz, my dear, we have been looking for you for quite some time now. You must come with us. What are you doing with these horrible vampires?" A tall lady with brown shoulder length hair her brown eyes stared down at me. She asked me as she had her hand out so I could hold on .

"Umm, yeah I am Liz, but I am a hybrid, I don't know where I belong," I said turning away in shame.

"Until you find that out you must come with us. You are a very special girl and very powerful. You can't stay with these vampires they are using you," she explained.

"Leave her alone you bitch, if she wants to stay with us she can," said Damien in a flash of anger as he held on to my arm and squeezed.

"Ouch, Damien, you're hurting my arm." I pulled my arm away.

"Sorry I didn't mean to," Damien replied.

I stood there trying to make a decision.

Meanwhile

"Tyler, I can't find Liz, why did you have to go and do that for?" Steven roared, at Tyler as he slammed the door shut.

"Because I don't want to be a vampire, maybe her lover vampires came and took her away," Tyler hissed back.

"You are being so greedy. You loved her before you found out. She is so young. Look at everything she has gone through. You can throw her away like that? I would have done anything to have her," said Steven.

"You can have her!" Tyler screams at him.

"Maybe I will if we ever see her again. She didn't ask for this you know, she needs support she needs friends not to be pushed away," Steven said as he looked around my living room. "We shouldn't be at Liz's house without her being here," Steven said as he stared at Tyler.

"Why not she won't care?" Tyler asked as he crossed his arms

"You are acting like a child, she is still Liz we still should respect her," Steven answered back as he stood up and headed for the door.

"Where are you going?" Tyler asked as he glared at Steven.

"I am leaving if you want to join you can if not that is up to you," Steven replied as he headed out the door.

"This is so fucked up," Tyler muttered as he stood up and went out the front door catching up to Steven.

Meanwhile

"Come on, Liz, you are running out of time," the wolf lady said.

"I think I will stay with Damien." I started walking away.

"Your choice dear, but the wrong one. Wait until they find out about you, it is just a matter of time and a war will begin," she said as she shifted back into a wolf and left with her pack.

"Why did you choose me?" Damien asked.

"Because I know you and I feel comfortable around you guys. Plus you're cute," I told him, laughing.

"Liz, you're too cute," Damien replied, smiling.

"I know. Bet you can't catch me!" I started running.

"Is that a challenge?" Damien ran after me.

I made it to the hotel before Damien and when I looked behind me he wasn't there. Ok I thought to myself.

"Damien where are you? You can come out!" I shouted.

"Liz, help!" Damien was yelling from a distance.

I ran toward his voice and saw that a pack of wolves was surrounding him.

"Enough let him go!" I yelled. My eyes turned red and I shifted into a wolf. My wolf form was bigger and stronger and I ran into the circle beside Damien and growled fiercely. The other wolves started to back off. As I began to turn away a wolf jumped on me and bit my neck, over and over again. There was blood everywhere and I started yelping. I knew I was stronger and I needed to be stronger. I dropped to the ground knocking that wolf off me then jumped on the wolf and bit down on his head. The wolf changed into a human and started pleading for his life.

"Liz, please no, we are sorry we will leave you two alone," The man begged, I slowly let him go and I shifted back into a human.

"Leave us alone," I said in a threatening tone.

"Yes, your majesty," The man said as he shifted back and ran away with the other wolves.

"Now let's get back to the room before we get into more trouble," I said shivering.

"Yeah, oh here you go," Damien said as he took his white muscle top off and handed it to me. .

"Thank I said," as I put his top on it was huge but it covered everything.

We made it back to the hotel, when we got there everyone was staring at us.

"Holy! Damien, did you get lucky?! I mean if you wanted some alone time with Liz you could have told us. You didn't have to leave," Conrad said laughing.

"I went outside looking for you two, but then I figured you wanted some alone time," Hunter explained.

"We didn't exactly get alone time," Damien answered.

"We were attacked by a pack of werewolves, the one wolf was a female and insisted that I went with them and that I was powerful, she didn't want you guys to find out," I explained. "Why didn't you go with them?" Hunter inquired

"Why? Do you not want me here?" I asked.

"You are very powerful and very beautiful. I do want you here," Hunter said.

"One thing weird though is one of the wolves called me 'your majesty'," I said.

"You are the alpha female. That is why they call you that," said Damien.

"So what happens now?" I asked, worried.

"We don't know who else is out there that may know about you. But you need to stay with us," Hunter replied.

"How can I trust you guys?" I asked as I shot Hunter a concerned look then glanced at Damien.

"Well, Liz, you can't, but I can give you my word that we are here to protect you," Damien explained.

"I still don't know what to believe or what to do, I am so lost. I never thought this would be how I would live my life as a hybrid, running away from vampires," I mumbled as I paced back and forth the room. I could feel another anxiety attack coming on so I stepped outside again to catch some fresh air I closed the door behind me and sat on the step.

"What are we going to do with her?" Damien asked Hunter.

"Give her some time, this is a lot for her to take in, she is so young, I will go talk to her," Hunter replied as he got up and went outside.

Hunter came outside and joined me. We stood there in complete silence, until Hunter spoke up.

"Liz, are you okay?" Hunter asked.

"I don't know, Hunter. I need some time." I started to cry.

"I know, but we are here for you," Hunter said

"How come you guys abused me if you really cared for me?" I asked as I turned and faced him.

"Because we didn't know how special you are we were scared of getting too attached to you I guess it was bound to happen at some point," Hunter explained, staring intently into my eyes.

I smiled a little, there was so much going through my mind it was overwhelming I couldn't stop thinking about how I was a hybrid and how come I just found out, and the biggest question is what was going to happen to me?

"You know Damien really likes you a lot," Hunter said.

"I know he does but what does that have to do with anything?" I asked.

"Well, he will always be here to protect you," Hunter explained.

"Hunter, have you ever wondered about me? You must have known I was a hybrid." I looked up at the moon in the dark sky.

"Yeah, sometimes but I was scared to meet you but I also knew that I couldn't run away for ever. And that this day would happen soon enough, and I am glad that I met you," Hunter replied.

"Why were you scared?" I asked. I was confused.

"Because, Liz, you are very powerful and you have no idea what you are capable of," Hunter explained.

"When will I find out how strong I am?" I asked as I stared into the night.

"When the time is right you will know. Now let's go back inside." Hunter opened the door and I sighed and followed him back inside the hotel room.

"I am tired, I am going to bed," I said yawning as I crawled into bed.

"She falls asleep fast," Conrad pointed out

"Yeah she does and she is so beautiful," Damien said as he cuddled in with me.

I woke up to a huge crash and bright lights and voices yelling. I was looking around but my eyes where having a hard time adjusting to the lights.

"Get the fuck back, vampire!" a voice yelled.

"What are you going to do about it, human?" Damien yelled.

"The bullets I have in here are wooden covered in a special plant called ivory that we found out that will knock you out, so does that answer your question you monster!" The voice yelled back. The voice was a deep scratchy sound it sounded like he had a constant frog in his throat.

Damien dropped to the floor, I looked around and all my friends where dropping to the floor like dying flies.

"Chad, watch out behind you!" Jack yelled as he tried aiming for me as I dove at Chad.

"No!" I yelled and got up and pushed one of the humans up against the wall. "What are you doing?" I snarled at the human as I pushed him harder into the wall.

All of a sudden I felt a stinging sensation in the back of my neck everything went blank and I dropped to the floor feeling paralyzed unable to move I was still able to hear everything that was happening around me I could hear those humans talking.

"Thanks," Jack replied as he sighed in relief.

"Where the hell did that chick come from?" Chad asked Jack as they picked me and tossed me on the bed.

"Put these other monsters in the van and you two guys drive back to the headquarters, I want to stay with her and find out some information," Chad ordered his army.

"Yes, sir," They all replied as they started to leave the hotel room.

"Jack not you I want you to stay with me," The man ordered Jack.

"Yes Chad," Jack replied as he locked the door

. I looked up at them both their 6 foot frame hovered over me. The one man had his brown hair tied back he looked down at me with brown eyes. I looked at the other man he ran his hand through his blonde short hair he took his broken glasses off and threw them down in anger he continued to stare at me with his green eyes.

The stuff that they shot me with that made me feel paralyzed must have been wearing off, because I finally had enough energy to realize what was happening and I shot straight up looking around. I was in a small room it was pure white the lights where really bright I could barely keep my eyes open.

"Where are my friends and what did you poison me with?" I as demanding to know.

"We took them away, sweetie and the stuff we shot you with is snake venom it acted like a temporary paralysis to calm you down. Now we're going to ask you a few questions and be a good little girl and this won't get nasty," Chad snarled at me as he came close to me.

"What do you guys want?" I asked as I snarled in his face.

"Hey, bitch, I said we ask the questions, not you!" Chad yelled and slapped my face violently.

I growled back.

"Okay, so there is our first question and I think you have answered it already you are a werewolf," Jack said as he wrote it down.

"Actually no I am not, you stupid fucks!" I kicked them in the face and made a run for the door the door was locked from the inside I was pulling on the knob trying to force it open. Chad got up and came right at me.

"You stupid bitch get back here!" Chad yelled and grabbed me and pinned me up against the wall he stood in front of me and hung on to me he stared me into my eyes.

"I wouldn't piss me off too much more if you know what is good for you, Chad," I hissed.

"Why what could this cute little girl do to us full-grown men?" Chad leered at me and licked his lips. I could tell what he wanted.

"I am more than a werewolf." I pushed him on to the floor.

"So you're the hybrid everyone has been talking about!" Jack clued in and his mouth dropped.

"Yeah, I am. What? You look disappointed," I said with a smirk.

"Oh no, baby, I am not disappointed, I thought the hybrid was a guy," Jack explained.

"Then you thought wrong. There is nothing stopping me from tearing you two humans to shreds so you're going to let me leave right." I turned and headed for the door.

"Actually sweetheart we do have something against you. If you leave then all I have to do is say the word and all your friends will be killed. I see that got your attention. So now let's get down to business." Chad stood up and looked at me with an evil grin on his face.

"Fine, whatever," I replied and crossed my arms.

"First of all you're coming with us and we are taking you to our friends, so get ready and let's go, baby," Chad said as he held on to my arm and he pulled a remote out of his pocked and pushed a red button that singled am alarm to open the door. He held on to me very tightly.

"You don't have to be so rough." I said as I glared at him.

"Yeah well if you wouldn't try and escape than I could trust you" Chad replied as we made our way out of the building and headed for the truck. Once we were at the truck Chad opened the truck door and pushed me in. Jack went to the back of the truck and reach in his duffle bag. He then came to the door and threw a pair of pants at me a belt and some sandals.

"Put these on if you want it might get chilly if you just wear that shirt, we won't complain if you don't," Jack said chuckling.

I didn't say anything I shot him a disgusted look and leaned back in my seat. I heard Jack on the phone it sounded like he was making meeting arrangements.

"Chad that was Blair he wants to meet him at this gas station up ahead we are going to hand over Liz," Jack explained.

"Sure thing," Chad replied as we pulled into a gas station up ahead.

"Honey get out, we're going to stop here. I am handing you over to my friends," Chad explained as we stepped out of the truck. I saw a man step out of the gas station he came closer. "Hey Chad, hey Jack, and this must be the hybrid?" A tall broad vampire asked as he shook Chad and Jack's hands.

"My name is Liz, and yes you are correct," I replied.

"Well, Liz, my name is Blair. I looked up at Blair he was really tall must have been around 6 foot 3 I would say, I could tell he was an older vampire due to some grey hairs peeking out from his brown short hair. He was wearing red sun glasses.

"Thank you I will take it from here," Blair said as he looked at me.

"You're welcome," Chad replied as they soon left and stepped into their truck and sped off.

"Follow me," Blair said as we walked towards a blue SUV.

Blair came over to the right hand side and opened the door for me I slowly crawled in, looking around there was only one other vampire in there. He smiled at me and stared at me with his brown eyes.

"Liz I would like you to meet Marty," Blair pointed out.

"You must be the hybrid?" Marty asked.

"Yeah I am," I said as I sighed.

"You are gorgeous," Marty replied.

"Thanks I get that almost every time," I said.

I started thinking again and every time I got into a deep thought I would get so pissed off. I hated my life, especially knowing what was in store for me. Why didn't my parents tell me? How could they fall off the face of the planet without letting me know what was going to happen? I mean school is obviously done for me now. My teachers probably think something terrible has happened to me. The police are probably looking for me. I had my life all planned out and it got ruined so easily. I don't have anyone to guide me through any of this. I looked around the van and let out a huge sigh everyone looked at me strangely. I ignored them and went back to my thoughts over running my brain. I snapped out it and I thought that I could try and make a conversation with Blair and Marty.

"So how come you guys were looking for me?" I asked hoping they would talk to me.

"What do you think you are the first hybrid and a female at that everyone will be looking for you," Blair explained.

"Yeah well I would like to get back to Damien," I snarled as I leaned back in my seat.

"Damien, you like him?" Blair asked as if he was surprised.

"At first I hated him, but now I don't know what to think," I replied.

"What I heard of Damien he is bad news," Blair said.

"Yeah I know and so is Hunter," I replied.

"There is a lot you need to know and understand you are living a different life now. We are here to help you but you need to help yourself to," Blair explained as we pulled over to the side of the highway I could feel the vehicle shake a bit.

"I know I am trying," I muttered to myself.

"I need to check something in the hood, my engine light is on," Blair said as he stepped out of the SUV and left it the hood up, there was bit of smoke that flew into the air.

"I am going to go see what is wrong with the SUV and if it is still driveable," Marty said as he stepped out of the SUV.

I stared at them wondering what was going to happen if we couldn't drive the SUV anymore. Then I noticed Marty he had a tribal tattoo going up his left arm and flowing up his neck, his brown short hair blew around in the wind, I noticed him not be too tall maybe around 5 foot 6.

"Shit I don't know what we are going to do I think I flooded the vehicle," Blair said in frustration.

"We will have to take the bus I guess, I think there is a bus stop in the next town and according to this sign we are only 15 minutes away," Marty said as he pointed at the green sign.

"Yeah I guess that is our only option," Blair said as he came around the SUV and opened my door. "Liz we need to walk to the nearest bus stop I flooded the SUV we will take the bus to Winnipeg our next stop," Blair explained.

"Alright," I said I wasn't too excited about having to take a bus.

We started walking in the ditch the wind was driving me crazy it was blowing my hair around and it was hard to walk against it.

"I am for sure going to lose weight walking against this wind," I said laughing.

"Yeah this wind is not helping matters," Marty replied.

My legs felt like rubber after making it the bus stop, there was a couple seats so I sat down and massaged my legs as I waited for Blair and Marty to order the tickets. A couple minutes later they walked up to me and handed me my ticket.

"It's going to be about a 10 minute wait," Blair stated.

"That is fine with me," I said as I looked at my bus ticket.

The bus pulled up and the three of us hoped on handed our tickets and sat in the very back. The bus was actually empty there was maybe three other people in the bus and they were up at the front. The bus made a squealing sound then the driver sped off turning back onto the highway heading for the Manitoba border.

Chapter Seven

THE TRUTH BE TOLD

"Liz, when did you find out you were a hybrid?" Marty asked quietly.

"A few months ago I found out I was a werewolf, then I was held captive by another group of vampires and that was when I found out I was part vampire," I explained.

"Do you know any of their names?'"

"There was Damien, Roman, Jeff, Conrad, and one I really like called Hunter."

There was silence for several miles and then Marty spoke up.

"Blair, don't you have a son named Hunter? And a daughter named Liz?" Marty asked.

"Yes I do." Blair responded.

"So does that make Liz your daughter?" Marty questioned as he glanced at me.

"I'm not quite sure yet" Blair responded.

"Did you even know where your daughter lived?" I asked Blair.

"Yes I do, in a small town called Prince Albert. I have never been there myself though. In fact, I have never met my daughter before," Blair explained.

Could I be Blair's daughter and could Hunter be my brother? And then I felt sick, if he is then I'm one weird chick for having a crush on my own brother.

"There is one thing I did give her though, there was a wolf statue. It carried a family secret that Jane and I put in it. Jane said she would pass it on down to our children so they would know what flows through their blood," Blair explained.

My heart stopped. "Oh my god! I have a wolf statue with a scroll in it and I'm from Prince Albert!" I blurted out I saw Blair's jaw dropped.

"That explains why you look so much like Jane. And it also explains why you are a hybrid," he said reaching out and gave me a big father hug. Blair just looked at me he smiled I could see the joy fill his eyes. It was kind of awkward meeting your dad for the first time especially after all these years thinking my father was dead.

"I can't believe I am reunited with my daughter I never dreamt of meeting you, I started hearing this story about a female hybrid being found I didn't believe it until Chad phoned me that is when I knew I had to meet you. So now here I am sitting beside the one and only female hybrid which happens to be my daughter," Blair explained as he continued to smile.

"I honestly don't know what to say I have gone so long without any parents, this is shocking news to me," I replied.

"I totally understand and you will probably need time to let all this sink in," Blair said.

"Yeah, but all the thinking in the world isn't going to change who I am and what I am," I replied.

"You're right about that, but you have to face the facts you are who you are. Anyways dear there is something I need to explain to you about the wolf statue your mother gave you and Hunter has a diamond hidden in it I am not too sure which one it is. This diamond is very dangerous as it holds the power to unleash a curse that is held amongst most vampires. This curse forbids vampires to walk in daylight. Now your mother kept it secret for many years but somehow they found out. And as we know, they will stop at nothing to get it back. What I am trying to say, Liz, is please hide that wolf statue because if this diamond falls into the hands of one wrong vampire it will be deadly," Blair explained.

"Why did mother hide the diamond in our wolf statues?" I asked.

"That is the only place she knew it would be safe," Blair said.

I didn't say anything I stared at the seat in front me, then I remembered how my wolf statue broke but I didn't notice any diamond. I didn't care about the diamond, all I wanted to know was if Hunter was really my brother.

"So does that make Hunter my brother, then?" I asked curiously.

"He could be, but I'm not really sure, I have not met any of my children until now. I guess if I ever meet up with this vampire you call Hunter I will be able to tell," Blair said.

"What are your plans now?" I asked him.

"I don't know yet," Blair replied.

The bus dropped us off at the bus station in Winnipeg. "The bus station isn't far from Mark's house," Blair said as Marty and I followed Blair. After walking four blocks we finally made it to where we were going for the night I wasn't sure where we were, all I knew is his name was Mark and I couldn't help but notice my legs being so cramped and this walk seemed to help the pain, after turning the corner Blair spoke up. "This is Mark's place he is expecting us, in fact he was expecting us a few hours ago," Blair explained as we stepped into the yard.. It was a smaller house and there weren't many tress in the yard, maybe a couple, I noticed some wind chimes hanging from the deck and the wind was making them chime like crazy. When we reached the door the light went off and I could hear a dog bark inside the house. Blair knocked and a deep voice answered it and let us in.

"Hello, my friends," A taller well-built vampire said as he greeted us and walked towards us.

"Hello, Mark," Blair replied.

I could smell vampires everywhere. The lights were dim and the vibe I got from all the vampires in this house gave me the shivers. The house was old there was a chandelier above us and in the corner before the stair case stood a huge white wolf statue the eyes were a bright yellow. The dog came up to me. It looked like a pit bull and it sniffed me and barked a few times but when I growled at the dog it ran away, his tail between his legs.

"Where is our hybrid? I am anxious to meet her," asked Mark.

"Right here," Mark answered, guiding me towards Mark.

"Well I never imagined our hybrid would look like this. Stunning, I must say," Mark said as he looked me up and down. I looked up at Mark I felt so short around all these vampires, Mark had to be at least 6 foot 1 well built his arms were like huge pipes, his brown messy hair it looked like he hadn't brushed his hair for days. I noticed a gold hoop in his left ear lobe his brown eyes never left me I noticed his face to be scruffy. I didn't care that we were in another house full of vampires and all I could think about was having a shower and getting washed up. I felt disgusting I needed a change of clothes and a good lay. I decided I should go and ask Marty but then I thought, what am I thinking? Mark would be way better.

"Can I have a shower?" I asked Mark.

"Well of course, I will show you where everything is," Mark replied as I followed him upstairs to the second room on the right.

"Here are the towels, and here is a nightgown you can wear, my dear," Mark said and left the room.

I jumped into the shower it felt so good to have a nice warm shower at last. I stood there letting the water run down my body. I dried off and brushed my hair ad slipped on the night gown that Mark gave me. I couldn't stop thinking about how Blair was my dad, and if Hunter might be my brother. I headed downstairs determined to learn more from my dad.

"Hey, Mark have you seen Blair?" I asked as I ran my fingers through my wet hair.

"Oh yea, lovely, he is over there." Mark pointed to the living room.

"She sure is something else," a shorter vampire said to Mark.

"Tell me about it," Mark replied, "especially in that nightgown mmm!" and licked his lips.

I found Blair and sat beside him.

"Dad, I feel kind of uncomfortable." I said.

"Did you just call me dad?" Blair asked as he looked surprised.

"Yeah," I replied.

"Okay, I wanted to be sure I wasn't hearing things? Why do you feel so uncomfortable?' Blair asked.

"Because I am the only girl and every male around here is staring at me, especially Marty. He gives me the creeps." I replied as I tried not to look at him.

"I know. Ignore Marty and stick with me and you will be fine." Blair replied.

"Is he like that with all the girls?" I asked.

"No, only the ones he thinks are pretty. And he has been waiting a long time to meet a hybrid," Blair explained.

I noticed Damien, Roman, Conrad, Jeff, and Hunter standing over by Marty and I got up and went over towards them.

"Damien what are you doing here?" I asked.

"Liz, we escaped those men and we found some gasoline over by an abandon car just outside of the building we started dumping it inside the building, I was just about to set the place on fire when one of the men yelled out that they would tell us where their boss took you. ," explained Damien.

"Oh so you were going to get you and the others killed just so they would tell you where I was," I said.

"We knew the fire threat would work so we weren't too worried," Damien replied.

"That makes me feel a whole lot better," I said sarcastically.

"Hello, Liz, don't you look stunning," Marty said and patted my ass.

"Don't you touch me!" I yelled and pushed him away.

"You bitch!" Marty yelled back and shoved me away. "Leave her alone," Hunter shouted and pushed Marty away from me.

"Why? What are you going to do about it?" Marty asked and laughed.

I looked at Marty and my eyes turned red I started shifting into a wolf. In my wolf form I am much fiercer than any other werewolf. My fur is white and I can stand on two feet. I become about 8 feet tall and have huge saber teeth. All the vampires in the room backed away from me but Marty stood there in front me with his mouth open. I reached out to Marty, grasped him by the throat and tossed him against the wall. I growled as he slowly tried to get up. I leapt and landed in front of him and tore at him again, growling all the time in his face. I stared at him for few seconds more before finally dropping in a heap on the floor. I looked around the room and then went upstairs. On the way I heard Hunter.

"Well Marty make sure you don't piss off the hybrid anymore," he said laughing.

"Fuck you, I was kidding. It wasn't my fault she took it to such extreme." Marty rubbed his head.

"You had it coming," Damien said.

In the bedroom I shifted back into a human and I sat on the bed crying I had no idea what had happened. I felt embarrassed even though I knew Marty deserved it.

Damien walked into the room. "Liz, are you alright?" he asked and sat down beside me on the bed.

"Not really. What happened there?" I asked, sniffling.
"You shifted into your hybrid form." Damien explained.
"I feel embarrassed." I said.
"Don't. You should have seen the look on Marty's face. It was too funny." Damien laughed.
"He needs to learn to keep his hands to himself," I said and wiping off my tears with a tissue.
"Yeah I know he does. Come back downstairs," Damien suggested and hugged me.
"Damien are these the vampires that are mean?" I hugged him back.
"Yes they are, but the leader is your father and I don't think he wants you to see you get hurt," Damien explained to me.
"Put some clothes on and come downstairs," Damien said.
I sat there for a bit slowly putting my clothing back on. I go back downstairs to join the party again, I felt nervous but I didn't really care anymore.
"Liz, that was awesome what happened," said Roman.
I overheard my dad talking to Damien about what their plans where for me..
"So, Blair, what do you plan on doing with Liz?" Damien asked Blair as he sipped on his drink.
"I don't know yet," Blair replied.
"I hope you don't have a soft spot for her because you found out she is your daughter. We still have to go through with the plan," Damien explained to Blair.
"I thought you cared about her?" Blair asked.
"I do, but I don't want to cancel the plans," Damien replied.
I was hurt and confused by their conversation. They both were startled when they finally saw me.
"Liz, what are you doing here?" Damien asked.
"I heard what you two were saying. I want to know what exactly are your plans for me?" I asked, anger rising in my voice.
"Nothing, Liz," my father replied.
"You are full of shit! Tell me now!" I shouted.
"Liz we will explain everything when the time is right, but for now forget about it," Damien piped back.

"Why does it matter? You guys don't care about me. You are trying to suck me in so you can get closer to me and earn my trust," I shouted at them and ran outside and leaned against the house, why must everything be so difficult and nobody tell me what the hell is going on around here?.

"Great, Blair, now she is going to run away again," Damien said and ran after me.

"Go away!" I yelled as I heard the door open behind me.

"Liz, can I explain myself?" Damien looked desperate.

"Fine, it better be good." I crossed my arms and turned to face him.

"Your dad and I have been planning something for when we eventually found you. Our plan is to discover if we can somehow use you to help create us vampires into hybrids as well."

"Why?" I asked crossing my arms.

"Because of you, you truly are amazing we could all live as one big happy family." Damien replied.

"But how are you going to create more hybrids?" I asked.

"We don't know yet," Damien replied.

"You mean it's not just about getting me pregnant?" I asked.

"That is what we thought at first, but that didn't seem to work so I guess we just have to keep trying and trying till it works" Damien smirked

"You would like that wouldn't you?" I laughed

"We are going have to talk to Caleb and this witch I know and see if they know anything"

"Who's Caleb and this witch you speak of?" I pondered.

"You will find out in due time, unfortunately," Damien replied as he glazed into my eyes.

"Well if you guys don't even know how to create these hybrids it could take a long time," I said and decided to go back inside. I was frustrated with everything and I wanted to breakdown and scream. All I could think about was ripping things apart and going on a killing rampage.

"Liz, I know you are frustrated but don't you like being around us anymore?" Damien asked following me back inside.

"Yes I do, but I want to live my life," I said.

I went and hid in the kitchen as everyone else was in the living room.

"You must be the hybrid everyone is talking about?" I heard a girl's voice ask me, I looked up and there stood a younger looking lady dressed in a white dress with long flowing blonde hair and blue eyes, she was thin but not too tall.

"Yes I am.I am Liz. And what is your name?" I asked, assuming there was no other girl here.

"My name is Emily. Are you scared?" she asked, all the while looking back to make sure no one was coming.

"A little bit. I don't know what they are going to do. Well I have an idea, but I don't know if I should trust them," I told her.

"I dated that Damien and he is an ass. He will suck you in and then one day he will snap," said Emily.

Damien interrupted us. "Hey Emily what are you two ladies talking about?"

"I am telling Liz how much of ass you are." Emily turned and walked away.

"Ha, don't listen to her, sweetie." Damien kissed my lips but I pulled away.

"Liz, what is wrong with you?" Damien asked me as he reached out to hold me.

"I am getting sick and tired of this shit. Please, leave me alone!" I pulled away from him and ran upstairs. And went into the bedroom and just stared out of the window.

"Where the hell is my daughter, Damien?" Blair asked Damien.

"She went upstairs. God, she is moody." Damien sat down on the couch.

"I will go and talk to her." Blair went upstairs.

I know who it was as soon as he opened the door, "I don't want to talk to anyone right now," "Liz, what is wrong?" Blair sat next to me.

"Everything, dad. What are you guys going to do with me?" I asked still looking outside watching the trees blow in the wind.

"We want to study you," Blair answered.

"Why?" I asked as I turned around to face him.

"Because we all want to be hybrids and you're the first," Blair explained. "And besides you are my daughter do you really think I would let anything bad happen to you do you think I would be able to live with myself, I love you Liz." Blair answered.

"Then why don't you want to tell me everything then?" I asked.

"Right now is just not the time and you have a lot on your plate as is." Blair replied.

"This is all so very frustrating it's starting to give me a headache and on top of that I'm getting really tired and just want to go to bed, where am I supposed to sleep?" I asked

"I am not sure we have to ask Mark," Blair replied as he seen Mark walk by. "Hey Mark!" Blair yelled for Mark.

"What Blair?" Mark replied as he came into the room.

"Liz is getting tired and she is wondering where she is supposed to sleep?" Blair asked Mark.

"She can sleep with me," Mark replied laughing.

"Whatever," I said rolling my eyes.

"My room is the last one on the right, dear," Mark said with a grin.

I shoved Mark and left the room and headed for his.

"What is wrong with her?" Mark asked Blair.

"She is frustrated with life," Blair replied.

I went into Mark's room and crawled into bed I fell asleep fast.

Damien comes upstairs to check what this going on the notices Liz isn't with the guys

"Where's Liz?" Damien asks as he comes into the room.

"She was tired so I sent her to my room to go sleep." Mark replied

"What the fuck Mark, what do you mean Liz is in your bed!" Damien yelled at Mark.

"Calm down Damien she was tired and I offered her my bed," Mark replied.

"Don't try anything with her she is mine!" Damien threatened Mark.

"Okay Damien, what makes you think she is yours?" Mark asked.

"Because, I said so." Damien stormed upstairs.

"What is Damien up to now?" Blair asked Mark.

I woke up to someone shaking me.

"W...what!" I yelled.

"What the fuck are doing in Mark's bed you slut!" Damien yelled at me and slapped me across the face.

"First of all I am in Mark's bed because I am tired, and second of all I am not doing anything with Mark so you have no right to call me a slut. And third, if you ever touch me again I will rip you apart. Mark is a better man then you will ever be!" "You bitch, you can have

Mark, he probably doesn't even want you. No wonder Tyler didn't want you!" Damien stormed out of the room and bumped into Mark.

"You probably heard everything I said in there. I don't care. You can have her if you want her." Damien snarled at Mark shoving him out of the way.

"Damien stop being an ass," said Mark.

"Liz, don't listen to Damien, Mark asked as he sat next to me.

"I wasn't worried about that, I am sick and tired of being abused," I told him.

Mark put his arm around me and I turned around to face him. He was really cute with his brown messy hair and handsome smile.

"Mark, will I ever have a decent life or will I be running all my life?" I moved closer to him.

"I think the first little while you will be running, but as time goes on you will be able to live a decent life." Mark moved the hair out of my eyes.

"Yeah I hope so, I feel like giving up." I could feel anger flowing through my body.

"Honey, I know this is a lot for you to take in." Mark kissed my cheek.

"Yeah it is. A few months ago I was still living at home and then overnight I was told I was a werewolf, and ever since I have been kidnapped and abused. That isn't a life for anyone."

"I know, but things will get better even if it doesn't seem that way, anyways I will let you be." Mark patted my shoulder and left the room.

Mark goes downstairs into the kitchen.

"Were where you Mark?" Blair asked Mark as he handed him a drink.

"I was talking to your daughter she needed someone to talk to. Poor girl is going through a lot, you know she needs more support," Mark explained as he took a sip of his drink.

I woke up and just laid there for a bit, I didn't want to be alone at this moment so I went out of the room and heard voices downstairs.

I went downstairs and was starting to get thirsty too so I went into the kitchen and noticed Mark and Blair in there talking.

"Hey, dad," I said as I walked past him and opened the fridge.

My dad ignored me. He wouldn't even look at me.

"Dad, what is wrong?" I asked.

"If you would talk to us about your problems instead of running away all the time things would be better all round," Blair said with an edge to his voice.

"Excuse me! If I am the one who's not good at showing my emotions!" I shouted.

I then go running upstairs into the bedroom where my jacket is and grab it and go

running out the door I had no idea where I was going but I ran and ran, I found a gas station and I went inside.

"Hey do you know where the nearest hotel is?" I asked the cashier.

"Yeah it's about 135 km south from here," he replied.

He then left me alone in the store and went outside to help a customer. I opened the till and stole some cash I needed some for wherever I was going and then quickly ran out before he realized what has happened. It sickened me that I had to do that but what other choice did I have.

I walked and walked the wind was a little chilly I could hear crickets chirping away. I was minding my own business mumbling to myself when I heard a truck pull over to the side of the road, I could have shifted into a wolf but I have no clothes for when I shift back into human form I am and didn't want to explain why I was naked to anyone.

Meanwhile Mark wanted to talk to Liz so he heads up to his room to see if she is still in his bed.

"Hey Liz," Mark said as he walked into the room and saw that I was no longer there, he went running downstairs. "Liz is gone!" Mark yelled.

"Fuck! When did she leave?" Blair panicked and went outside.

"A while ago I think." Mark followed Blair.

"I can smell her scent she can't be far," Blair explained. "We have to go after her," Blair demanded.

"Why, she can take care of herself?" Mark asked.

"She is at that stage where she will get out of control she doesn't care at this point she will draw attention to herself," Blair explained as he smelt the surroundings.

Meanwhile I stood there waiting for the person to step out of the truck. Finally a tall man about 6'3, fairly built stepped out of the truck he stood there staring at me it was awkward.

"Hey do you need a ride?" he asked as he tipped his hat showing his brown receding hairline.

"Yes please," I replied as my eyes lit up.

"Well hop on in," he said as he opened the door for me and then got into the driver side.

"What is your name, dear?" he asked and looked at me inquisitively with his brown eyes.

"Liz," I muttered.

"My name is Jay. So where are you going?" Jay asked.

"To the nearest hotel," I replied.

"What is a young little lady doing out so late by herself?" Jay asked me.

"It is a long story." I said as I stared out the window.

I was starting to get hungry all I could think about was his blood, I could hear his blood pump through his veins. I looked in the back seat all I noticed stakes and crossbows back there.

"What are those back there?" I asked Jay although I knew exactly what they were for.

"You wouldn't believe me. You would think I was crazy if I told you." Jay was laughing.

"Try me. I bet you hunt vampires," I said looking at him in the eyes.

"Yes! How did you know?" Jay asked me and looked at me with fear in his eyes.

"I can tell by all the crossbows and stakes back there," I answered.

I could see that Jay was getting suspicious that I might be a vampire.

"So, you do believe in vampires, then?" Jay asked, still staring at me.

"Yes. And werewolves," I replied.

"Werewolves, have you ever seen one?" Jay asked as he turned into the parking lot of the hotel.

"Yes, I have," I said getting out of the truck. "Thanks for the ride," I said and closed the door.

I checked into a room and sighed.

"Stop right there honey and turn around slowly," It was Jay. I knew even before I turned to face him.

"I am a cop, and I know what you are, and I know what you have done. Face the wall and spread your legs. You have the right to remain silent," Jay said and mumbled on.

I let him cuff me. I thought did he find out I robbed that gas station, I wonder what he meant by done, although I did find it kind of a turn on having a cop brush his hands all over me. "Come on baby, you are coming with me," Jay said as he pushed me back into his truck.

"Jay, do you actually think you are going to get away with whatever plans you are trying here?" I asked as I stayed calm.

"I know you are a vampire and I know what your kind does. I torture vampires your kind killed my family you sicken me," Jay snapped as he back handed me.

I growled a bit and slowly turned my head to face him. "I am more than a vampire honey, I am a hybrid and there is nothing stopping me from tearing you apart right now," I glared at him and my eyes turned red.

"You are the hybrid? I heard about you through another vampire I killed. Why don't you kill me then?" Jay waited. I didn't answer so he came to the other side of the truck and opened the door and helped me out. I could tell that he was scared, he was shaking so much that he dropped the handcuff key on the ground. I decided this was the moment for my escape. I shifted into a werewolf, determined to kill everything in sight. I roamed around in wolf form all night, I could hear people screaming. I started howling, I could hear other wolves howl back at me. I collapsed when I got shot with a couple of tranquilizers. I woke up the next morning in a car and had a splitting headache,

"Hey, hot stuff you're awake." I heard a man's voice.

I had no idea what was going on but I could tell that a car had pulled over and that someone was carrying me into a building. I was surrounded by lots of men, they were humans but I couldn't smell any vampires or werewolves. The lights were so bright I could barely keep my eyes open. I hear a squealing noise coming from the ceiling fan and it was bothering my ears.

"Well, well if it isn't the wolf girl," he said as he touched my face.

"What do you want?" I asked. I could barely breathe.

"We want to know everything. You see we know what you did, and let me tell you, you sure are a bad wolf and you need to be punished" Kevin replied and knelt down in front of me and his brown eyes stared into mine. I noticed a wolf a tattoo on his left arm and wonder if there was a connection with it and this place.

"You already know what I am, so what else could you possibly want and need from me?" I tried getting up from the chair.

"Leave me alone with her!" Kevin shouted at the rest of them.

"You're foolish leaving yourself in here with me," I warned.

"Oh honey, you can't shift. I drugged you so I can do anything I want to you," Kevin replied as he position his 6'2, 195 pound frame in front of me.

"So, tell me, where is your family? I know there are more of your kinds out there. Where are they?" Kevin asked.

"I don't know, I left them and as far as I know I am the only hybrid." I don't like the idea of humans getting involved.

"I wish you wouldn't lie to me, sweetheart," Kevin said as he picked me up, I did manage to grab some of his brown hair before he threw me down on the ground. He crawled on top of me, his knee crushing me in the chest. "You little bitch" he slapped me across the face really hard," He then whispered in my ear. "Lying will only get you killed too."

Kevin stood up, laughed, and kicked me with all his strength in my side. His boots were heavy. He left me lying on the floor, gasping in pain.

"Someone else go in there and torment her for a while, I am exhausted," Kevin demanded to one of the other guys.

"I will. I heard the door open and then close, I could hear footsteps getting closer. I looked up and there was a man standing over me, a big smirk on his face. His 6 foot frame leaned over me he pulled my arm and forced me to stand up then pushed me on the chair again.

"My name is Brett I am going to get down to business. Talk little girl!" Brett snapped at me as he took a black comb and ran it through his blond thin hair. His grey eyes glared into my eyes. I stared at him I wanted to rip his throat out. I could see him talking but I wasn't paying attention.

"Hey I am talking you're going to start listening," Brett snapped.

I spat in his face. I knew that would make him even more pissed off with me but I didn't care. He slapped me across the face then got up and walked around me.

"You're going to talk to me, whether we do it the easy way or the hard way it is your choice," Brett said as he put his fingers through my hair, ready to pull.

"What do you want to know?" I asked.

"Are there any more like you?" Brett demanded as he sat down in front of me.

"Not that I am aware of," I answered.

"Where is your family?" Brett asked as he grabbed my chin.

"I left them, I don't know where they are, I've already answered these questions. Don't you have anything different to ask me? It doesn't matter how many men ask me the same questions there will always be the same answers" I tried to pull face away from his hand.

"Oh don't be like that. You sure have a big mouth on you for such a tiny girl and you know what I think, I think you know where your family is," Brett said as he kept putting more pressure with his hands that where on my face, he then forced me to stand up from the chair.

"I don't, I swear. I had a fight with my dad. My boyfriend and I ran away!" I pushed his hands away, shoved him across the room and ran to the door quickly opening it and ran down the hallway. I could hear voices everywhere. I could hear that man yell at the other men.

"Get that little bitch!" I heard someone yell down the hallway.

I was about to turn the corner when a hand yanked me into the a side room.

"Liz, shhh! It's Hunter," Hunter said to me as he tried to calm me down.

"Hunter, oh I missed you guys, how did you get in here? Where is everyone else?" I asked as I hugged him so tight he could barely breathe.

"Liz you're hugging me too tight. I pretended to be a guard and the others are outside," Hunter replied as he peeled me off him.

"Sorry, I am excited to see you, I am sorry I ran away. But how did you know I was here?" I asked.

"I could sense you. You are my sister and I can always tell where you are," Hunter replied as he looked around the dark storage room to see if we could use anything to help us escape.

"Sister? What are you talking about?" I asked as I looked at him with confusion.

"Blair told me the whole story and I found out he is my dad and that you are my sister. I had a wolf statue like yours." Hunter kissed me on the cheek.

"Okay, now we need to figure out how to get you out of here," Hunter said as he was looking around the room. "I think I have an idea. Follow me," Hunter guided me out the door and into the hallway.

"There she is, the little bitch!" Kevin said as he reached for me.

"Kevin, let me take her. I found her. I need some words with our little hybrid," Hunter demanded as he took me away from Kevin.

"Okay, but be fast about it, and make sure she tells you everything," Kevin said as he let me go.

Hunter then brought us both to the exit and quick as possible and we were able to get out of there.. We met up with Blair, Mark and Marty and we all piled into the van as quick as possible. We then sped away, couldn't get away from that place quick enough.,

"Liz, what the fuck do you think you were doing you could have had got yourself killed? You can't be exploiting yourself like that to the whole world those men are very bad people," Blair had tears in his eyes.

"I am sorry, dad, I couldn't control myself," I explained as I was looking around to see who else was there.

"Next time we might not be here to help you," Blair said.

I didn't really know what to say so I stared at the floor of the van.

"See, the little bitch is a trouble maker," Marty said from the backseat.

"Marty, shut the fuck up. Who asked for your opinion?" said Mark.

"Oh, Mark what now? So you are in love with her?" Marty said, laughing.

"No, you're mad because you didn't have your way with her, and she embarrassed you," Mark replied.

"Shut up," Marty said and glared at me.

"Where is Damien and Jeff ?" I asked looking around.

"They are at my place waiting for us," said Mark.

We soon got to Mark's and we all piled out of the van. I was so tired I knew I was going to fall asleep as soon as I hit the pillow. When I entered the house I got an uneasy feeling, I couldn't see Damien or

Jeff anywhere and the hairs on the back of my neck where standing straight up.

"Liz don't move," Hunter said as he brought me closer to him.

We turned on the lights and saw that the house had been destroyed and there was no sign of Damien or Jeff.

"What the hell happened?" Mark asked as he looked around his once beautiful house..

"I don't know, and I don't know where Damien or Jeff is. We have to leave." Blair said.

I was trying to smell my surroundings to see if I could track down anything, but no luck. Whoever did this knew what they were doing. I kept walking to see what I could find, I couldn't smell anything but I knew there would be something we could work with, if only we could find it. I looked all around me and then in the far distance I noticed something tied up to a tree and I could smell blood so I went running. And there was Damien, barely moving. He opened his eyes and was agitated. He tried to speak. He was trying to warn me, but I couldn't make out what he was trying to say. I almost had him untied when I was hit over the head with something, falling to the ground and unconscious. I soon woke up in a hotel room, but I didn't recognize anyone there.

"Hey toots your finally awake," A voice said to me as I looked around the room.

"Who are you ?" I asked as I was trying not to fall asleep.

"I am your worst nightmare, unless you cooperate," he replied as he came closer to me.

"Can we do this in the morning I am very tired and bitchy?" I said as I closed my eyes, he didn't seem very scary so I didn't care.

"I must not be scary if she can fall asleep," he replied.

"Fine, but first thing in the morning you need to answer some questions, now get your beauty sleep," he said as he got up off the bed.

I didn't even hear what he was mumbling on about.

I woke up and I had no clue where I was. I jumped out of bed; it was dark and hard to see I kept backing up and backed up into someone.

"What are you doing awake, hun?" the guy asked as he held onto me.

"I can't sleep anymore, and I need to use the washroom," I replied as I moved away from him, I slipped into the washroom. When I came out the lights were on and he was sitting on the bed. He pulled out a chair for me to sit on, I sighed and went and sat down.

"So what is your name?" he asked me.

"Liz," I replied.

" Liz hmmm, if you must know my name is Dallas that's what name you can scream when I'm fucking your brains out" Dallas replied I just rolled my eyes like I haven't heard that before.

Dallas was cute he tried to act tough but he wasn't really good at it. He was too much of a pretty boy with his nice little goatee and blond hair, his blue eyes shone in the light. "Why am I here?" I asked looking at him.

"I need to ask you a few questions. Do you know anything about the hybrid? I need to find him," Dallas asked as he stared at me as he straightened his 6'4, 215 pound frame out to look intimidating.

"Why, are you going to hurt him?" I asked as I started to shake. I could smell that he was also a vampire.

"No, I want to see him for myself," Dallas replied.

"I don't know where he is," I said as I stared at the ceiling.

"You're lying!" Dallas yelled and hit me across the face. He then grabbed my hair and slowly started ripping out strands of my hair.

"No stop! Okay, I will tell you, please stop," I begged.

"I knew you would be a good candidate and tell me," Dallas replied.

"I am the hybrid," I said looking at him..

"How can a little girl be the hybrid? Then your dad must be Blair. Your mother must be Jane. And your brother is Hunter?" Dallas asked looking shocked.

"Yes, now can I leave? I have to find my family." I got up from the chair.

"Not so fast little girl, you need to prove to us that you really are the hybrid, for all we know you could be lying to me." Dallas shoved me back down on the chair.

I rolled my eyes.

"Fine!" I yelled and started to shift. I stood there in my werewolf form growling at them. I then shifted back into human form. I realized I had no clothing on so I grabbed a blanket and wrapped around my body.

"Wow, you really are the hybrid," Dallas said as he came closer to me and touched my face.

"Yes, now since I told you the truth can I go now?" I asked as I held the blanket closer to me.

"Ha, honey you actually think you are going anywhere, I finally found you?" Dallas pulled the blankets away from me.

"Hey! Give me the blankets back." I grabbed them out of his hands.

"No way, honey." Dallas pinned me on the bed.

"Dallas I wouldn't do that if I where you.

"I want to make you mad it turns me on to see pissed off female" Dallas started to undo his pants.

"Get off me! I don't need this shit right now!" I chucked Dallas across the room.

Dallas got up, he was really angry now and he grabbed me by my hair and pushed me onto the floor.

"Ouch, Dallas, what the hell!" I tried to stand up.

"Listen here, bitch, because you are the hybrid it doesn't mean that you can get away with anything that you want. Do I make myself clear?" Dallas now held me by my throat.

I couldn't breathe so I nodded. Dallas finally let go and I gasped for air.

"Okay, sweetheart, you are going to come with me he said as he held on to me.

"Where?" I squirmed to try and get away.

"You will see, honey," Dallas said.

He took me outside to his car it and shoved me onto the passenger seat.

I did what he asked me to even though I could get away. But where would I go? I had no idea where anyone was.

" Dallas I need some clothes, and girl stuff," I said as I started blushing.

"Oh, ok we will take you to a store," Dallas replied as he turned into a mall parking lot.

Dallas then got out of the car and went to get Liz to come in.

"I'm not going in with a blanket," I said, "You need to shop for me" Dallas went into the store.

He then comes back to the car about 15 minutes later with a bag in his one hand and hands it to Liz.

"Thanks Dallas," I said as he gave the bag of stuff.

"You're welcome," Dallas replied with a smirk on his face.

I open the bag and find an oversized bright yellow shirt, a pair of blue jogging pants and some brown sandals. He except me to wear this?

"Dallas where is my women stuff and you want me to wear this crap, I'm a female not a clown." I said.

"I didn't know what you meant by women stuff and I would wear that so I figured you would too." Dallas replied.

"Let's go back in and I will show you exactly what I need ok." I said.

I then put on this clothing if that's what you want to call it and proceeded to go into the store with Dallas. We went into the fashion section and I got a nice knee length black dress that came with a black lace bra. We then went to the shoe section and I got a nice pair of brown flats. I then took Dallas over to the pads and tampon area and showed him what I meant by lady stuff. His face turned a bright red and said, "You really wanted me to buy those?"

"Well yeah," I replied smirking.

We then proceeded to the checkout, I grabbed a bottle of water on the way there and then went up to the till, Dallas paid for everything then I went to the bathroom and changed into some clothes and didn't make me look like sun. I came out of the bathroom with my new outfit and Dallas just whistled and said "Ohhh sexy."

"Does this look better than what you got me?" I asked as I twirled around.

"Oh yeah big time" Dallas answered.

We then went to the car and I threw the other clothes onto the back seat. I didn't know where we were going but at least I was looking pretty going there.

A couple of miles down the road I turned to him and asked, "What is going to happen now?"

"There is someone that wants to meet you," Dallas replied.

"Joy I can't wait," I said sarcastically.

"You know Liz, it must be hard for you to understand what is happening to you," Dallas said as he started driving.

"Yeah, it is. I guess I have to go with the flow of things," I replied as I rolled down my window.

"Yeah that is all you can do, I mean things will get easier in time," Dallas replied as he lit up a cigarette.

"I suppose it will. Say, are humans trying to start a war with vampires and werewolves?" I asked as I turned my face away from the cigarette smoke.

"I don't know what the humans are trying to do, I try and stay out of their way" Dallas said as he put his cigarette out and turned the radio on.

"So, Dallas, do you have a girl friend?" I tried to start a conversation with him.

"No I don't. Do you have a boyfriend?" Dallas asked.

"I don't know anymore, I did a few days ago but we had a big fight." I felt tears flowing down my face thinking about my family, I quickly wiped the tears off my face so I wouldn't have to explain why I was crying.

"That is too bad, he probably regrets it," Dallas said as he kept on looking at me.

"My boyfriend was the one you guys tied up to the tree and left to die," I hissed as I crossed my arms.

"Oh shit, Iwas trying to send out a message," Dallas explained.

"Well it worked, it caught my attention that's for sure," I replied as I started to doze off.

I woke up in a bed and had no clue that I fell asleep for that long. I got out of bed and went to the washroom. I could hear voices outside the hotel, but I couldn't make out what they were saying, I was still way too tired to comprehend the conversation. I went back and laid down but there was no way I was falling back asleep again so I laid there staring up at the ceiling.

"Liz, are you awake?" Dallas asked as he came over and lay beside me.

"Yes, how long was I asleep? And where are we?" I rolled over to face him.

"For about five hours, and we are in a small town on the border." Dallas kissed me.

"Alright," I said as I lay still in complete silence.

I stared at him, he was attractive in his own way but seemed confused by what was happening. He leaned towards me and kissed my lips gently and I kissed him back. We stared into each other's eyes and kissed some more. I pulled away and stood up, and headed for the washroom. I didn't feel right about being with another vampire yet. I stepped out of the washroom and Dallas was laying on the bed looking at me.

"What is the matter, did I do something?" Dallas asked and smiled.

"No, I don't feel right about being with another vampire, not yet," I got up to get dressed.

"I know, Liz you are so beautiful I will wait for you," Dallas said and stood up.

"I wouldn't want you to wait for me," I replied.

"I know, but it is my choice," Dallas started to make the bed.

Back at Mark's place the other vampires are slowly trying to figure everything and get everything back in order. They bring Damien into the house and lay him down on the bed and Mark and Marty keep on looking around for Jeff while Blair tends to Damien.

"How is Damien?" Hunter asked Blair He is doing a bit better, he will still need to get a bit more rest," Blair explained to Hunter as they poured themselves some wine.

"I miss Liz, we must find her," Hunter said as he took a sip of his wine.

"I know I miss her to, I don't even know who took her," Blair said as he sat down on the couch in front of the fire place.

The door then open and Mark and Marty come in with Jeff right behind them.

"Looky, looky who we found wandering in the woods," Mark says.

"Jeff what the hell happened?" Blair questions him

"A vampire barged in destroying everything it seemed like he was looking for something. The vampire spotted Damien but took off into the forest as for Damien he grabbed him and tied him to that tree where you guys found him. "I need a drink to relax," Jeff said

The guys were sitting down and one of their cells began to ring.

"Whose cell phone is that?" Blair asked as he looked around the room.

"Mine I will answer it," Jeff said. "Hello", Jeff said with a serious look, as he put down his glass of wine.

"Hello, is this that little hybrid's family?" The guy on the other line asked.

"Yes, what did you do with her?" Jeff asked the man.

"Oh nothing yet, but if you want to see her alive again, I suggest you find that diamond that I am looking for, you have 24 hours boys the clock is ticking," the man on the line said and hung up the phone.

"Fuck, fuck, fuck!" Jeff yelled as he slammed the cell phone down on the floor.

"Jeff what is going on?" Blair asked Jeff as he went over to him.

"I didn't catch who he was, I don't think we know him, but he said that he has Liz and he will kill her if we don't give him the amulet in 24 hours," Jeff explained as he turned to face Blair.

"Well no more wasting time, let's go find Liz," Blair said as the guys got up and headed out the door.

THINGS KEEP GETTING WORSE

"So Dallas what are we going to do now?" I questioned him.

"You will see, sweetheart, it is a surprise." Dallas answered.

I giggled and followed him outside and we hopped into the van and took off down the road. He soon turned into a long drive way and stopped the van, not that far from the hotel. The house looked like it hadn't been lived in for a while, the trees in front of the yard looked dead.

I followed him inside the house. The door was unlocked so we stepped in, as we were waiting I scoped out the house it was fairly big, it smelled like flowers, there were paintings of nature all over the place and there was no carpet black and white tile.

"Nice to see you, Dallas," A tall well-built man came from one of the rooms and hugged Dallas.

"Nice to see you to Caleb," Dallas said hugging him back.

Caleb is this the Caleb I warned about? I thought to myself as I tried not to make eye contact.

"Who is this fine young lady?" Caleb asked as he stared at me with his brown eyes, and the look on his face was like he was going to rape me right there and then.

"My name is Liz," I replied and I backed away.

"Nice to meet you," Caleb said as he whispered in my ear. "I know you are the hybrid and I will keep you here with me, because I am the male hybrid," Caleb said has he smiled at me.

I didn't know what to say. A male hybrid. This could be interesting. "Why don't you two come into the living room with me?" suggested Caleb.

We followed him into the living room I couldn't help but notice how tall he was he was so muscular he could just pick me up and pin me to the bed and hold me down with one hand, his brown hair was everywhere it looked like he has never heard of a comb. I was really uncomfortable, I didn't know what to think at this point. Caleb was cute but he was also creepy, he kept staring at me in a sexual way and the vibe I got off him was scaring me. He smiled at me as he ran his fingers through his goatee.

"Dallas, I am scared," I said as I cuddled in with him.

"Why?" Dallas put a reassuring arm around me.

"Because Caleb said I was his and because he is a male hybrid." I replied.

Dallas was speechless. I saw that Caleb heard what I said. He glared at me.

"Liz why don't I show you around my place," Caleb suggested.

"Sure I guess," I replied.

"Ok, go meet me in the kitchen I will be right there," Caleb demanded.

"Alright," I said as I sighed and stood up I went into the kitchen. I was looking around waiting for Caleb to step in any minute, the kitchen was big the counter was made from marble and there was an island in the middle of the kitchen also made from marble bar stools surrounded the island. I was standing there and the hairs on the back of neck stood straight up I turned around and Caleb was right there.

"You scared me did you have to sneak up on me like that?" I asked as I took a step back.

"I whispered that in your ear for your information only, Liz!" Caleb snarled at me as reached at my clothes. He pulled down my pants.

"No, please I am sorry." I started to kick and scream.

"Shut up, bitch, you are getting punished!" Caleb covered my mouth with his hand. He struggled but managed to get his pants down and with a few grunts he forced himself on me.

"Was that necessary?" I asked as I pulled up my pants.

"I did it to punish you. You are a sexy thing I must say." I shoved him out of the kitchen and I headed back into the living room to find that Dallas was lying there dead on the floor.

"What did you do to him?" I yelled as I ran over there to see if he was alive, but he was gone.

"He couldn't know what I was, I don't want anyone else to find out, you were foolish to tell him," Caleb replied as he picked Dallas up and put him in a coffin and sealed it shut

"Why couldn't he know, he knew about me?" I asked as I felt hatred for him.

"You see my dear vampires, werewolves and especially humans should never know our existence, because we are very special and powerful. Too bad for you though more than enough vampires know about you already you have no hope," Caleb explained.

"What do you mean, they are my family they won't hurt me," I snapped.

"You are naïve I wish I could make you think otherwise," Caleb replied as he came closer.

"Get away from me, my family is all I have," I snarled.

"For now until they run tests and lock you away and give you to the humans," Caleb announced.

"Why would they do that exactly? You know what don't answer that I don't believe you," I hissed as I headed for the front door.

" Where do you think you are going?" Caleb asked with a serious tone.

"I am going home, no offense but you scare me," I answered as I shook my head.,

"I don't think so, you are staying with me, you shall be my wife," Caleb said as he smiled at me.

"You wish," I said reaching for the door knob, but before I could open the door Caleb stepped in front of me he squeezed my hand forcing me to let go of the door knob..

"If you ever try and pull that stunt again I will have no choice but to hurt you, my love!" Caleb locked the door. "Now get up and get ready for bed," Caleb said as he helped me up.

"You can't force me to stay with you!" I yelled.

"Oh you bet I can dear, you see I bribed your family, if they don't arrive here in a few hours with that diamond they will think that I killed you," Caleb explained.

I ran into the kitchen to see if I could get a sharp object to hurt him for a bit so I can plan an escape. I grabbed a knife and stood there waiting for him to come at me. Caleb came around the corner and when he saw me standing there he smiled. The tension between us was so thick you could cut it with a knife, he stood there, I stood there then finally he came over to grab my arm. I had my hand behind my back I quickly stabbed him in the chest, he cried out and fell to the floor, I took off running, not looking back, and ripped the door off the hinges, there was no way I was about to play around with a lock when a psycho hybrid was after me. I could hear him screaming in the background but I kept running.

"Liz you bitch, you can't escape!" Caleb came running after me.

I shifted into a wolf and ran, unfortunately for me I ran right into the middle of the road and got struck by a car. I laid there and shifted back into a human all I could hear was voices.

"Oh shit, hey lady are you alright?" A voice asked me as they checked my pulse to see if I was alive. "Hello, yes there is this lady lying in the middle of the road, she has been hit by a vehicle," the person said on the phone.

I woke up in the hospital I was in so much pain I could barely stand it. The doctor came in to check my vital signs and to check my blood pressure.

"Hello, miss, I am Dr. Gerald, how are you feeling?" Dr. Gerald asked me as he checked my iv bags.

"I am okay, in pain though," I replied as I looked around the room.

"Ok I will give you some pain medication, in the mean time you should try and get some rest," Dr. Gerald explained.

I couldn't sleep I had many thoughts running through my head. I looked around and noticed someone talking to the doctor outside of my door . I stared by everything was still blurry, I couldn't make out who was it was so I listened to try and figure it out.

"I am her brother, doctor. I can take care of her at home," Hunter explained.

"No, I am sorry I can't let you do that, she needs her rest," Dr. Gerald reassured him. "Now if you will excuse me I need to do some more tests," "Of course you have to do things the hard way!" Hunter growled and pinned the doctor up against the wall and bit his neck. Dr. Gerald screamed and collapsed. Hunter then came over and removed all the tubes and iv bags and carried me to the van. I didn't say a word I was too weak, I thought I would heal way faster than this.

"Go!" Hunter yelled at Jeff to start driving.

"I don't understand why she isn't healing properly, she should have been healed by now," Mark said in distress.

"I think because she isn't drinking enough blood, I have seen this happen before when a vampire doesn't get enough blood they slow down on their healing, they get weak." Conrad then made a phone call.

They carried me into a friend of Conrad's and laid me on the couch. I couldn't even open my eyes I was so weak and exhausted.

"Thanks, Trent, for letting us stay here. She is very sick," Conrad put a warm cloth on my forehead.

"No problem, what is wrong with her?" Trent asked Conrad.

"She got hit by a vehicle and she is not healing very well." Conrad explained.

"Has she been drinking blood?" Trent asked.

"I don't think enough," Conrad replied.

"Here I have a lady friend who will give you some of her blood and we will see if that helps." Trent beckoned his friend over.

"Cassandra love can you feed Liz some of your blood?" Trent lifted my head up.

"For you Trent, yes!" Cassandra cut her wrist and her blood dripped into my mouth. I opened my eyes. The blood tasted so good I wanted more, I jumped off the couch and held Cassandra up against the wall and bit her neck I couldn't stop myself.

"Liz, stop! That's enough!" Trent screamed as he came over and threw me back onto the couch as Cassandra fainted on the floor.

I snapped out of it and lay there looking at Conrad and Trent, I then started crying.

"I am sorry, I didn't mean to." I started crying even more.

"Liz it's okay, as long as you're okay. How do you feel?" Conrad asked me as he wiped the tears off my face.

Trent picks up Cassandra and lays her on the couch.

"Give her time to get her strength back," Trent said as he wiped the blood from Cassandra's neck.

"Conrad can you take care of Liz for a few days, we are going to take off we have some stuff we have to deal with?" Hunter asked as he stood up and looked at the boys.

"Yeah, Trent and I can handle it from here," Conrad replied.

"Okay, we will let you know what is happening," Hunter said as he came over and kissed my fore head.

"Good bye for now," I said with a look of content.

"We will be in touch in a few days," Hunter replied as I heard them leave.

"How are you feeling?" Trent asked as he touched my cheek.

"I feel a bit better, still a little weak," I replied.

"Get as much rest as you need, I will take you to a bedroom Liz," Trent said as he carried me upstairs and he laid me on his bed. "We will be downstairs if you need anything," Trent said as he covered me up and he left the room.

Trent went downstairs and seen Conrad in the living room.

"Is she sleeping?" Conrad asked Trent.

"Not yet but I told her to get some rest," Trent replied.

"Is she your girlfriend?" Trent asked Conrad as he turned the fire place on.

"No, I do care for her though," Conrad replied.

"She is the hybrid if I am not mistaken?" Trent asked Conrad.

"Yes she is, and she doesn't know how to control it," Conrad replied.

"I can see that, she will learn," Trent replied as he looked up at the clock.

"Yeah, I mean poor girl she recently found out she was a werewolf, and now she is a hybrid that is a lot to comprehend," Conrad said as he got up to fill his glass up with more wine.

"I know, but she will have to get used to it, and unfortunately if the wrong person finds out that could be the end," Trent explained as he looked out the window.

"Yeah I think she knows. Are you expecting company?" Conrad asked Trent as he looked up at the clock to see the time.

"Yeah, some of my friends are coming over, we are going to play poker and have a few drinks would you like to join?" Trent asked.

"No I think I will pass, I am going to go have a rest," Conrad replied as he got up and went upstairs.

"Suit yourself," Trent said as he opened the door to let his friends in.

"Liz are you awake?" Conrad nudged me.

"Yeah, I can't sleep." I sat up. "I have been awake for some time now just lying here," I said as I rubbed my head.

"I was worried about you. So were the others," Conrad moved closer.

My heart started racing. Was Conrad coming on to me? He was hot was so cute I didn't think he liked me that way.

"Yeah, I was worried too." I replied as I took a deep breath in my ribs were still in pain though. "Ouch it hurts to breath," I said as I touched my side.

"You almost got yourself killed. You need to start feeding more," Conrad explained as he lifted my shirt up to see if I bruised.

"I know, I find it so hard though, I hate hurting other people." I replied as I jumped a bit when he touched my side.

"I am sorry dear if that hurts I will leave you alone," Conrad said as he pulled my shirt down and looked into my eyes.

"Conrad I really like you," I told him.

"I really like you too, Liz," Conrad held me tighter.

We both laid down Conrad had his arm around me and cuddled me. I eventually fell asleep in warm arms. I woke up a few hours later and Conrad wasn't with me anymore. Conrad came out of the kitchen holding a drink and was about to go back to the bedroom when he heard Trent's voice. He went into the living room where everyone was.

"Where is Liz?" Trent asked.

"She is still sleeping," Conrad replied as he looked around to see who all was there.

"Is Liz that hybrid everyone has been talking about?" A lady asked Conrad.

"Yes, she is," Conrad replied as he sat down on the couch.

"Can we meet her?" The lady asked Conrad as she sat beside him.

"Not tonight Chantal, she is sleeping," Conrad replied.

I come into the entrance of the living room, "No I am not," I said as I stood there looking quit annoyed. "You guys are loud remember

I am a wolf to," I snarled as I looked over at the girl who was staring at me intensely. Even a blind person could tell she was staring. Her black long hair covered half her face, her red sparkly dress hugged her small frame her brown eyes stared at me and then she smiled her red lipstick brought out her white teeth.

"Hi I am Chantal. Wow I can't believe I am actually meeting the hybrid, you're so beautiful," Chantal said to me as she came closer to inspect me.

"Yeah, thanks, now if you excuse me I am going to grab myself something to drink," I said as I wandered into the kitchen.

"I'm sorry if I was being a creep it's just I heard a lot about you and your so beautiful." Chantal explained as she poured me a glass of wine.

"Thanks," I replied as I took a sip of my wine even though I didn't really care for it and wandered back into the living room.

There was a lot of vampires around, but no sign of my brother, my father or Damien. I sighed and sat down on the couch.

"Hey, honey, what is wrong?" Conrad asked me and put his hand on my lap.

"Conrad why are you touching the hybrid bitch?" Another lady screamed at Conrad across the room.

Everyone stopped what they were doing and starred at her. She came stomping over towards him and grabbed his arm and slapped him across the face. She stopped and glared at me and tried to slap me . I grabbed her arm before she could do anything and I pinned her up against the wall and growled at her.

"Don't touch me or Conrad ever again because I will rip that pretty little mouth off of your face, darling," I growled t her as I threw across the floor and she slid into the counter and banged her head against the counter. She got up slowly feeling embarrassed everyone was looking at her. She rubbed her head confused on what just happened.

"How are you so strong I am lot older then you?" She asked surprised.

"I am a hybrid, so don't piss me off!" I glared at her.

"Well, bitch, Conrad is mine so lay your slutty hands off of him," she yelled at me she picked up a knife off the counter to stab me with.

"No, Sandra, she is stronger than you!" Trent yelled at Sandra to stop.

"Not a chance this bitch is dead," Sandra snapped as she bolted towards me.

I turned around just in time and I grabbed her wrist and twisted it until she dropped the knife. She screamed in pain.

"I told you not to piss me off didn't I?" I held her up by her neck and stared into her blue eyes, her dirty blond hair hung over my hand.

"Let her down, she isn't worth it," Trent said.

"Fine, have it your way, she is a waste of a vampire anyways," I snapped as I threw her petite body across the room.

"I'm going to back upstairs, I am too bitchy at the moment," I stomped away back upstairs.

I was upstairs sitting on the bed anger filled my veins oh how I wanted to rip that bitch apart. I sat there just thinking of how I could have so much anger inside me I was so frustrated of what I have become. I stood up and looked at black hanging mirror that was attached to the door I stared at it for a few moments and screamed at myself I punched the mirror and shattered it into a million pieces. I looked at my hand blood poured down my arm and onto the floor I watched the cuts heal almost immediately. I went to washroom and cleaning up I was surprised no one came running upstairs I would of thought for sure they would have heard that loud smashing sound of the glass breaking.

Meanwhile downstairs Sandra is pacing back and forth pondering of how she is going to get me back.

"Do you actually like that psycho bitch?" Sandra asked as she stopped in her tracks and looked at the boys.

"Actually yes I do, and that psycho bitch is my best friend's sister." Conrad replied as he have Sandra a cold look.

"If that little hybrid bitch thinks she can get away with making me look like a fool she has another thing coming to her," Sandra hissed as she crossed her arms.

"Just leave it Sandra," Trent said as he took a sip of his wine.

"No she pissed me off and that is it," Sandra replied.

"Ok Sandra but we warned you," Trent stated.

"I am not scared of a big bad wolf," Sandra said as she laughed a bit.

After cleaning up I felt more calmed down so I went back downstairs, I swore to myself if that bitch tried anything again I would tear her throat out.

"Hey Liz what were you doing?" Conrad asked as he winked at me.

"I was just calming my nerves," I replied as I smiled at Sandra.

"You really do think your all that just because you are a hybrid well bitch let me tell you something I have been around a lot longer than you have so you better get rid of that attitude or?" Sandra hissed I cut her off before she could finish.

"Or what I am so scared what will you do to me nothing so don't even threaten me!" I snarled as I stared into her trembling eyes.

"That is it," Sandra muttered as she slowly turned around and grabbed a glass that was left empty on the coffee table and snuck up behind me and smashed it over my head. I turned around and chuckled picking the glass from head.

"Why did you do that?" I asked as I pushed her up against the wall. "I am going to give you one more chance that is it after that your life in on the line you hear me!" I yelled at her as her feet dangled she struggled to get loose. I let her go she fell to the floor.

"I am not giving up without a fight," Sandra said as she slowly got up and slammed me up against the wall and hit me a few times.. I stood there I turned around and growled I started to shift into a werewolf.

"Good job Sandra you really pissed her off," Trent said as the others moved out of my way.

Sandra stood there looking terrified. I went up to her and growled in her face I slapped her across the face so hard that she went flying across the room and slammed against the other wall. I then took off after her she pleaded and begged for me to stop. I grabbed her and sank my teeth into her head blood poured down her face. I stopped and dropped her and shifted back into a human. I forgot that I was naked and I stood there looking at the dead Sandra.

"Oops, I didn't mean to do that," I said as I giggled.

"That is alright, Liz, she had it coming. But you're naked," Conrad passed me a blanket.

"Oh shit, I forgot." Embarrassed, I put the blanket around me.

Trent said, "Guess I'm volunteered to clean up this mess thanks a lot," as he looked at me.

"You would have done the same thing if you were in my shoes she got under my skin," I said as I continued to look at her lifeless body as Trent started cleaning up my mess.

I went upstairs and went to the bedroom and got a change of clothing then went and had a shower.

Back downstairs Conrad watched as Trent finished cleaning up.

"That was quite a show," Conrad said as he looked at the dead Sandra.

"Yea it was, I can't believe the wolf she changes into," Trent answered.

"I know she is scary but she has so much power but doesn't know how to use it," Conrad said.

"I know I can see it in her the strength just begging to come out," Trent replied.

"What do we do with Sandra now?" Conrad asked as he stared at the huge gash in her head.

"I don't know just drag her downstairs for now," Trent said as they both lifted her up and hauled her to the basement.

Meanwhile I got out of the shower and dried myself off and put on some clothes and then opened the bathroom door. I walked towards the bedroom when I noticed Conrad and Trent heading up the stairs I slid into the bedroom and tried listening to their conversation then Trent turned around and saw me.

"Hey there you are," Trent said as he came towards me.

"Hey Liz, how was your shower?" Conrad asked.

"Good it was relaxing," I replied.

Trent stared at me the whole time, he lusted over me big time. Conrad noticed that about Trent and the fact that he stared at me all the time.

"Trent, do you mind?" I asked laughing.

"Sorry Liz," Trent said as he smirked.

I was starting to feel really uncomfortable around him especially with all the other vampires around here to.

"Conrad, when can we leave? I miss everyone."

"Probably tomorrow." Conrad answered.

"Alright," I replied as I went into the kitchen

There were a couple of other vampires one short and stalky with brown curly hair the other one was tall and slim with red shoulder length hair in the kitchen when I went in there, I ignored them and went into the fridge and got a glass of blood, they both looked at me.

"Hello, you must be Liz," the red head asked me.

"Yes I am," I replied as I took a sip of the blood.

"I am Carter and this is Cameron," Carter said as he looked me over.

"Hello, nice to meet you two," I said as I headed back into the living room. "By the way Carter I like your red hair," I said as I smiled at him.

"She likes me," Carter said.

"Give it up," Carmon said as he made a pouting face,

"She is hot," Cameron said to Carter.

"I know, I would have that any day," Carter said laughing.

I heard every word they said about me and shook my head and kept walking.

"Liz, are you ready to leave?" Conrad asked.

"I thought you said tomorrow?" I asked confused. Something didn't seem right I had a really bad feeling and I hate it when I when have bad feelings because I am always right.

"Yeah, but we can leave now." Conrad replied.

"Okay, I will go get ready," I replied.

"Okay, I am going to go tell Trent that we are leaving," Conrad said.

I went upstairs, I knew they wanted to be alone, while Conrad talked to Trent.

"Trent, Liz and I are leaving now. Thanks for you for letting us stay here," Conrad said to Trent as he stepped closer to the stairs.

"You're not going anywhere, Liz is mine," Trent hissed at Conrad as some of the other vampires wearing black ski masks and padded vests grabbed Conrad so he couldn't move.

"What, I should have known you were up to no good," Conrad snapped and tried fighting the vampires off, but they were too strong. Then one of the vampires shot Conrad with a stun gun Conrad screamed and he fell to the floor in pain.

I was lying on the bed thinking about things, I was too lazy to move. Finally I budged and got up slowly making my way downstairs.

"I am ready to go," I said as I ran down the stairs. I stopped dead in my tracks and looked around there was no one in site. I could tell that there was something wrong. I knew it I knew my instincts where correct.

"There you are my dear," Trent opened a door and approached me.

"Trent, where is Conrad? And what is going on here?" I asked as I slowly backed away.

"Oh, love, Conrad is downstairs being tortured and as for you I am going to make you mine," Trent said laughing.

"Really not this crap again," I hissed

"You really are a turn on baby when you get mad like that, but unfortunately for you I am much stronger than you think." Trent came closer to me.

"Now, Trent, what are you going to do with me?" I ran towards the basement door.

"Oh I have lots planned for you, my dear," Trent said as he shoved me downstairs.

I flew right into another vampire and landed right on top of him.

"Ouch, fuck that hurts," I growled as I got up from the vampire.

"You can stay on me the entire time baby," the vampire said as he got up.

"You wish," I growled I got up and rubbed my neck I looked around the room to see if I could spot Conrad.

"You will never escape," the vampire guard stated as he got up from the cement floor.

"I wouldn't be so sure," I hissed as I scoped the room some more. I could feel someone behind me.

"Looking for him honey?" Trent pointed out Conrad as he grabbed a knife and stabbed him in the chest.

"No stop, please," I screamed.

"Oh what is the matter, Liz, you can't stand your lover getting hurt?" Trent stabbed him again.

"No, please I will do anything!" I was trembling in fear.

"Oh, honey, I know you will." Trent dropped the knife and approached me. He pulled my hair and dragged me all the way upstairs. When we got upstairs he pushed me on the couch and forced himself over me. I was kicking and screaming but managed to push him off and I ran towards the stairs but before I could open the door Trent grabbed me and threw me across the floor into the kitchen, I hit my head on the counter was knocked out when I woke up a few hours later I was locked in a cage, I slowly got up, my head hurt like a 3 day hangover.

"You're awake, Sleeping Beauty," Trent said.

"What happened, why am I in here?" I rubbed my aching head.

"You hit your head pretty hard on the counter, then you passed out and I put you in this cage so you wouldn't escape." Trent replied.

"Are you going to keep me in here forever?" I looked around.

"Not forever. But until you can prove to me that you won't escape." Trent replied chuckling.

"I will never be yours," I hissed at him.

"You know, Liz, I don't know why you have to make this so difficult. Why can't you cooperate and do as I say?" Trent knelt down in front of me.

"Because you disgust me, Conrad and I will escape." I said as I spit at him.

"You don't fucking get it, do you? Your lover boy doesn't really love you in fact he is on my side. He used you, Liz," Trent stood up and looked at his watch.

"You are a lying bastard and if he is on your team then why are you torturing him?" I snarled I tried to shift into a wolf but for what reason I couldn't.

"Ah my dear you can't shift I bought a potion from a witch that will stop your transformation until it is out of your system," Trent explained.

"You asshole if Conrad really was using me then why are you torturing him?" I asked.

"To let you think he was on your side, this was all planned ," Trent said as he left the basement.

I had no idea who to trust anymore. How was I going to escape and be free? I kept asking myself as I looked around in the dark cold basement. I noticed there were figures hanging on the walls, they had machines attached to them, I wonder if those where the human they feed on. I could hear voices coming closer I knew it was Trent by his smell he had this spicy smell to him.

"Get lost why don't you kill me it would be better than being here?" I snarled.

"Honey don't be like that, I am going to let you out for a few hours to have play time if you are a good girl maybe longer," Trent said laughing as he unlocked the door.

"Stop treating me like I am an animal!" I shouted as I bolted passed him pushing him into the door.

I ran upstairs there were vampires everywhere.

"Oh shit," I said as I looked around.

"You must be Liz, the escape artist," One of the vampires said as he scoped me out.

"Yeah, and I am pretty good at it," I hissed back as I crossed my arms.

"If you are so good at it, then why do you always get caught?" Trent said as he came up from behind me, sending shivers down my spine.

"Because I always trust the wrong crowd." I replied.

"Whose fault is that dear?" Trent asked.

"What the hell are you doing?" I asked.

"Liz, I am going to make this very clear, if you do anything stupid I will kill your friends and family," Trent said as he picked me up and shoved me against the wall right into a mirror the mirror to break into tiny pieces all over the floor. My body ached from being shoved around and thrown into things.

"I wasn't going to," I said as I tried to push him away.

"Good, Simon, go free Conrad," Trent summoned Simon. Simon was Trent's main guard I noticed all of his guards to wear ski masks it was difficult to tell them apart.

I watched Simon go downstairs, and a few minutes later come back up with Conrad following close behind.

"Hello sweetheart," Conrad said as he came closer towards me.

"Get the hell away from me you sick fuck," I yelled and spat in his face.

"You bitch, we should chain you up with the other human in the dungeon and hook you up to our blood circulation machine so we can keep sucking you dry over and over again. Have our fun with you anytime we feel like it. " Conrad said as he pushed me down on the floor. He pinned me down so he could have his fun with me but I spotted a shard of the broken mirror beside me, I managed to grab it. I stuck it into Conrad's back.

"Fuck you, bitch!" Conrad yelled as he tried to grab it out of his back. In the mean time I got up and ran out of the house all the guards were chasing after me. I shifted into a wolf and ran, and ran and ran. I was pretty sure I lost them for now, where to stay was another question. I finally made it home. That was the nice thing about being a werewolf, we are superfast. I jumped through a window that was left open, shifting back into a human I went upstairs and had a shower. I dried off, got into some cozy clothing and crawled into bed. I was so exhausted I felt like I haven't slept in days I could feel my body get limp as I closed my eyes. I soon woke up and went downstairs I was so thirsty but who was I kidding? I had no blood in my house. I figured what should I do I thought maybe I should go for a walk and she if I can find someone to feed one. About a block away from my house I spotted some punk trying to break into someone's car.

"Hey lady do you have a smoke," the punk asked me as he stopped what he was doing and came towards me. I stared at him he had tons of earrings in his left ear and nose ring, his hair was black and spiked up his black leather jacket had a few tears in the arms and his blue jeans where all torn up, his laces on his black boots where untied and dragging on the road. I couldn't stand the smell he gave off he smelt like cigarettes and garlic.

"No I don't smoke," I replied as I kept walking.

"Oh that is too bad, what is a pretty little thing doing out so late?" the punk asked me as he tried to grab me.

"You shouldn't have done that I was going to let you live," I snarled as I pushed him into a tree, then bit his neck, he only screamed for a bit, I dropped him and then wiped my mouth off and went back home. I closed the door and felt like someone was watching me.

I screamed, "Now what the hell do you want now," getting ready to shift.

"Liz, it's me, Roman," Roman said as he shot me a worried look.

"Roman, where have you been?" I hugged him.

"I was trying to find you," Roman said as he hugged me back.

"Where is everyone?" I asked.

"They are on their way. We were so worried about you," Roman explained.

"I know I was really scared, Roman, I don't know who to trust anymore." I started to cry.

I wondered over to my couch and slowly sat down Roman came and sat next to me.

"What happened?" Roman put his hand on my leg.

"After you guys left, Trent and Conrad tried to rape me. It was horrible." Through the window I noticed bright lights pull up in my driveway.

"What? Conrad betrayed us? Wait until Hunter hears about that.," Roman was shocked, "We didn't know Liz." Roman said as the boys walked in.

"Hunter, Damien, dad, Mark, and Jeff," I yelled as I went running over to them and hugged them all.

"Liz, are we ever glad to see you," Hunter said with a big sigh of relief on his face.

"How are you feeling, Damien?" I asked

"Better. Thanks for asking," Damien answered

"What happened? Where is Conrad?" Blair asked as he took his jacket off.

"After you guys left Conrad and Trent became really evil. They tried to rape me and took me hostage, who knows what they would have done," I replied.

Blair says, "Feels like there is still more."

Also before all this happened, I didn't mention anything about Caleb he is the male hybrid and he raped me, he is the one that tried bribing you with the diamond." I explained as I could feel the anger pulsating through my veins again. Blair came over and held me to try and comfort me.

"I am going to kill that asshole!" Hunter said as he threw one of my lamps across the room.

"Hunter, I know you're angry but can you try not to break my stuff?" I asked as I giggled a bit.

"Oh, sorry," Hunter replied as he went over to the broken lamp and picked up the broken pieces and placed it on my end table.

"What happened to this Caleb you speak of?" Hunter asked looking concerned.

"I don't know I stabbed him and took off, I didn't think twice about it," I explained, thinking about it gave me the creeps.

"Well he will probably be looking for you, my dear," Jeff spoke up.

"Where is Conrad now?" Blair asked as they followed me to the living room.

"I don't know, I stabbed him and took off running," I replied

"I'm tired and worn out, I need to get some sleep," as I started to head back to my room.

"Go and get some sleep, we'll be out here," Hunter said

"Ok, night" I said as I went to my room and got into my bed. It didn't take me long before I was out like a light.

Hunter and Blair come into the room to check on Liz.

"I can't believe how much this poor girl has gone through," Hunter said as he touched my forehead.

"I know and it is the start of it too. She will never have a rest," Blair replied.

"I also can't believe my best friend would betray me like that to and even think about hurting my sister," Hunter said as he started to get angry all over again.

"I know I sure didn't see it coming," Blair answered.

"How come you guys left her, I mean you guys are her family?" Roman asked as he approached the doorway.

"We weren't sure if she was a werewolf or vampire, we never even thought she would be both and we didn't know how we would tell her, so we gave her out for adoption," Blair explained .They left the room and Blair quietly closed the door. They headed back to the living room.

"When I first met her I found her to be extremely attractive until I found out she was my sister, I mean I still find her pretty but I don't think of her that way," Hunter explained.

"Yeah I was an asshole towards her when I first met her, back when she was dating Tyler but the more I hung out with her the more I found myself to be drawn towards her," said Roman as he sat down on a brown love seat.

"I think we were all a little hard on her," Hunter replied as he relaxed on the brown easy chair.

The next morning I woke up trying to figure out where I was at first and then it all came back to me I was finally home. I remembered everyone was in the living room so I rushed out and seen everyone still sleeping. I was so glad that I was back with my family again. I went into the kitchen and got a glass of water. I could hear movement in the living room and next thing I know someone was behind me.

"Good morning, Liz." Hunter put his arm around me.

"Good morning, Hunter," I replied as I took a sip of my water.

"Liz, you know we can't stay here, it's too dangerous," Hunter explained and back into the living room. I didn't know what to say, I thought we could all be a family and stay here.

"What do you mean it's too dangerous?" I asked Hunter, following him into living room.

"Well, Liz, Conrad and Trent are probably still going to be looking for you and until they are killed you are not safe." Hunter headed for the stairs.

"My life will never be safe"

"That is true, but please try not to run away," Blair replied sounding serious.

"Well stop aggravating me, " I replied as I went upstairs.

"She sure has an attitude, like her mother did at that age," Blair said as he laughed.

"Hunter, where are you?" I shouted as I went into my room. I saw Hunter on my bed. "Hunter are you okay?" I poked him.

"Yeah, Liz, I am fine," Hunter got up.

"Okay, making sure, I am going to have a sandwich then we can decide where we are going," I said as I went into kitchen..

"Hey Hunter are you alright?" Roman asked Hunter as he looked around my room.

"Yeah I am fine, a lot on my mind lately," Hunter replied as he rummaged through my stuff and started putting stuff in a bag.

"I am going to look through her drawers too," Roman said as he held up a pair of pink thong underwear.

I walked into my room as Roman was showing my underwear off to Hunter.

"Hey, Roman, cut it out!" I grabbed them and put them back into my dresser.

"Geeze, Liz, it was just a joke," Roman replied.

"I know, but Hunter was probably disgusted, he is my brother." I snarled as I put my hands on my hips.

"I don't know about that," Roman said as he left the room.

What did he mean? I thought to myself as I look at Hunter.

"Hunter, what did Roman mean by that?" I asked.

"I feel embarrassed, but Liz I know you are my sister, but I find you extremely attractive I can't help it." Hunter replied.

"Wow Hunter, you said that very well. I don't know what to say." I replied as I giggled.

"I have never seen a female hybrid before, and when I first laid my eyes on you I couldn't believe how gorgeous you were" Hunter explained as he hugged me.

"Thanks, I am glad you are my brother." I said as I hugged him tight.

"I will always protect you, Liz," Hunter kissed my forehead and then went downstairs.

I put my hair in a ponytail, zipped up my bag and went downstairs to join the others.

"Holy! What were you two doing upstairs?" Roman asked.

"Nothing, I was getting ready and Hunter was keeping me company." I replied.

"Liz, go get some better clothes on, you are not leaving with us like that," Blair demanded.

"What is wrong with this?" I asked looking sternly at Blair. "It is too sexy, Liz. That is what is wrong with it. You already have problems keeping the boys off you," Blair explained.

"Fine, you're treating like a little child." I stomped upstairs.

"She sure is something else," Roman said as he looked out the window and saw a car pull up.

"What is it, why do you keep looking out the window?" Blair asked.

"There is someone here, I can't tell who though," Roman replied as he turned to Blair.

"Who would be coming here, no one knows we are here," Blair replied as he was trying to peak out the window.

"I don't have a clue but whoever they are they are wearing hoods, and they are coming up to the front door," Roman replied as he started walking towards the door.

There was a knock at the door.

"I will get it," I yelled as I went flying downstairs and opened the door. I stood there in shock. It was Conrad and Trent.

Chapter Nine

THE CHALLENGE

"Hello, baby," Conrad said as they both stepped into my house.

"I could use a little help!" I yelled.

"Leave her alone," Hunter tried to push me out of the way and into safety.

"No way, we are taking her. We missed her," Trent said.

I couldn't help but have thoughts about tearing their faces off and watch them bleed on the ground.

"Why don't you give up?" Roman stepped in front of me trying to protect me.

Trent reached in his cloak and grabbed a stake and staked Roman in the heart.

"No!" I yelled I could feel the anger pulsating through my blood, I could feel my bones break and my hair grow and teeth getting sharp. The look on their faces was priceless as I stood there and growled in their faces.

"Holy shit we have really pissed this chick off," Trent said as he backed up a bit.

I jumped on Trent and bit his face, I could hear him scream, I felt so strong, I clawed open his shirt I sunk my teeth in to his chest and ate his heart. I had no idea how I managed to be that strong, and howled. I then felt myself shift back into human as I collapsed to the floor. I had used too much energy.

"Get her a blanket," Hunter said.

Blair came back with a blanket and wrapped me up in it. "You fucker, how can you betray us?" Hunter yelled at Conrad.

"It was the only way I could stay alive. Trent would have killed me," Conrad explained.

"Why should we trust you?" Hunter snapped as he had Conrad by the throat.

"I don't except you to," Conrad replied as he struggled for air.

Hunter growled and released his hand from Conrad's throat. Conrad took a big breath in and rubbed his neck. Blair just shot Conrad a dirty look.

"I don't think Liz will ever have a normal life," Blair said as he kissed my forehead.

"No, and the worst is yet to come," said Hunter.

"What do you mean?" Conrad asked, looking at Hunter.

"There are more dangerous vampires out there than us, and they are coming for her, I can feel it," Hunter explained as he stood up and carried me over to the loveseat and laid me on it. They all went into the kitchen to let Liz rest.

I got up a little while later and I rubbed my eyes then looked at Hunter who was sitting on a chair staring at me.

"What time is it, what happened?" I asked as I got off the couch.

"It's two in the afternoon, and I am sorry Liz but Trent killed Roman, you shifted into a wolf and killed Trent then you collapsed," Hunter explained as he looked at me.

"Roman is gone?" I asked as a tear ran down my face.

"Yes," Hunter answered as he hugged me.

I got up, and went to my room and got dressed, did my hair then I went downstairs and saw Conrad sitting on the couch.

"What the fuck are you doing here?" I said as I ran in front of Conrad.

"I am sorry, Liz, I didn't mean to hurt you. I was trying to keep myself alive," Conrad said.

"You tried to rape me." I said in an angry tone.

"Because I wanted to show Trent that I didn't care about you," Conrad tried to explain.

"Oh," I said, "but I still don't trust you" as I sat across from him. "Where is everyone anyways?" I asked as I looked at Conrad.

"They went out somewhere, they didn't mention where but still it would only be for a few minutes," Conrad replied as he leaned closer to me.

I had a bad feeling about Conrad he still seemed untrustworthy and up to no good. Conrad got up and came over to me and held me down on the chair.

"You're a weak little bitch, I can't believe your brother trusted me with his smoking hot sister," Conrad said as his one hand ran up and down my body..

"You're an asshole I knew you were up to no good." I tried squirming away.

"You're hurting my feelings honey," Conrad unzipped his pants.

"Why can't you guys come up with something different to do?" I asked as I shoved Conrad against the wall and bit into his neck. I watched the bit marks slowly turn purple he held onto his bit marks and slid down the wall he just stared at me. "Good bye," I said as I went and sat on the couch and continued to watch as he slowly died.

I heard the door open and saw Hunter come walking through the door. Hunter saw Conrad laying on the floor his neck was purple and blood dripped down his neck and surrounded him on the floor. Hunter walked towards me and looked at me.

"Are you ok Liz?" Hunter asked me.

"Not really," I replied as I looked up at Hunter. "He tried raping me again I had to do this," I replied as I stood up.

"I am sorry I left you with him by yourself," Hunter apologized as he hugged me.

"You didn't know where is everyone else?" I asked as I stepped away from Conrad some more.

"They are coming in shortly, just parking the van" Hunter explained to me.

"Why is Conrad acting like this?" I asked Hunter.

"I have no idea Liz," Hunter replied as he nudged Conrad to see if he was conscious.

"He is gone a werewolf bite is fatal towards vampires," I explained as I stood behind the couch.

"I know it is I just wanted to make sure," Hunter replied.

"Anyways Hunter I am going for walk," I said as I turned around and headed for the front door.

"Stay out of trouble," Hunter replied.

"Yeah, yeah, yeah," I replied getting on my shoes and opening the front door. I stepped outside and stood there smelling my surrounding. The fresh air was such a nice smell. I started walking down the block just taking my time when I saw a strange man with brown curly hair leaning up against a white picket fence near a park. He saw me and his eyes lit up.

"Hey sorry to bother you miss, but do you have a dollar?" The man leaning up against the fence asked "No, I am sorry I don't," I replied and started walking away.

All of a sudden before I could even blink, there were about 10 vampires jumping out of a huge van. They surrounded me and pointed their guns at me.

"Ok boys drop your weapons, you're scaring our poor hybrid," That same man that asked me for a dollar demanded the vampires.

"My, my, I didn't get a very good look at you in the park, you sure are a pretty girl Conrad wasn't lying," The man said as he touched my hair.

"You must be Kelvin," I said shaking as I stepped away his 6 foot frame was menacing but sexy in the same way, his brown eyes felt like they were undressing me.

"Conrad told you about me, I see. And yes that is correct dear," Kelvin said as he brought me into a school bus, do I even want to know what they did to get this.

"I killed Conrad," I hissed as I sat down.

"That is alright he told me how to get you that is all I care about," Kelvin replied smirking.

"Let me guess you are going to attempt to rape me?" I asked as 'I refused to look at him.

"Well baby that doesn't sound like a bad idea, what do you think boys?" Kelvin asked as he looked around laughing hysterically.

I rolled my eyes and looked out the window. I just stared out there wonder what was going to happen next. I thought back to all the good times I had before all this mess happened then I started thinking about everyone and wondered what they were doing.

"I wonder where Conrad found you," Kelvin said as stared at me.

"Damien introduced us," I said with a regret.

"Why would you assume that we were all going to rape you?" Kelvin asked.

"Because most men try" I replied.

"I probably am going to have a hard time resisting," Kelvin replied as we pulled into a drive way.

I rolled my eyes once again. I peeked through the bus window the house was white and had a pond in front. I kept looking at Kelvin he was extremely attractive I never had this sort of attraction since Tyler, and Damien. The attraction I feel with Kelvin is much different it's stronger and very strange.

"This is my place," Kelvin said as we stopped the bus and we made our way out. As soon as we stepped out the driver took off with the others. I looked around it was nice and well-kept birds where swimming in the pond the sound of their whistling was soothing. We walked inside there was a red carpet that flowed down the hallway his house smelt like cinnamon and ginger.

"Kelvin, why does your house smell like spices?" I asked as I gave him a strange look.

"I like to bake just because I am a vampire doesn't mean I can't cook or bake," Kelvin replied as he smiled at me.

I giggled a bit as we headed for the kitchen. The kitchen was very spacious the island was enough for at least five settings. Every appliance was stainless steel and in one of the windows I noticed a huge vine plant crawling up the window.

"Nice place," I said as I continued to look around.

"Thanks, would you like a drink?" Kelvin asked as he opened his cupboard and reached for a couple glasses.

"Sure," I said rubbing my stomach.

Kelvin reached into his fridge and pulled out a bag of blood and poured us each a glass of blood. I chugged mine like it was going out of style. I handed my glass back to Kelvin and wiped my mouth off. He was standing there giving me a surprised look.

"Someone was hungry," Kelvin said as he took the glass from me.

"Yeah I was," I replied.

"Let's go into the living room," Kelvin said as we walked into the living room

I was amazed it was gorgeous. The carpets where white the furniture was a white leather over in the corner by the television were a 90 gallon saltwater fish tank. His television was at least a 50 inch just hanging on the wall. We sat down and silence took over a few seconds, I couldn't take it anymore so I spoke up.

"How did you hear about me?" I asked as I faced Kelvin.

"Conrad was one of my best vampires him and I talked a lot and when he met you he couldn't wait to tell me," Kelvin explained.

"I am sorry I killed him it was getting too much to deal with," I said apologizing and turning the other way.

"It's ok I really don't blame you. Conrad was aggressive and he didn't know when to stop," Kelvin explained.

We ended up talking and laughing and for hours the more I talked with him the more I seemed to get closer with him. Eventually I lunged at him and straddled him I started kissing him he kissed me back his hands were up my shirt. I couldn't stop I wanted more.

Chapter Ten

THE UNEXPECTED

Kelvin then picked me up and laid me down on the couch he undressed then undressed me. His hands wondered my body. He started kissing my whole body eventually making his way up to my lips again. I wrapped my hands around his neck and pulled him closer he then entered me. I moaned and arched my back. I could feel myself pulsating I scratched his back as I did that he moved faster.

"You're so sexy," Kelvin said as he slowed down. He laid on my for a few seconds before getting off.

"You're to," I replied smiling.

"Let's go upstairs I am going to shower then we should get some rest," Kelvin said as he swept me off the couch and carried me upstairs. He brought me to his bedroom and placed me on the bed kissing me one last time before he left his room. I slowly sat up looking around his room. The bed was a king size with red covers a white rug covered his floor there was a brown cedar chest at the edge of the bed leaving his room smelling like cedar. I got off the bed and made my way to the bathroom. I could hear the shower so I slowly opened the door and swung the shower curtains open.

"You scared me, what are you doing?" Kelvin asked.

"I wanted to join," I replied as I hoped in with him.

We started washing each other's bodies we stood there letting the water run down our bodies. We washed up and dried off. I ran to the bedroom and got underneath the covers. Kelvin joined shortly after. I fell asleep in his arm. I woke up and I thought it was later than what it was the sun was shining in my face. I looked up at the clock and read 7:00 am. I tried to shut my eyes again but a hit of nausea took over. I jumped from the bed and ran to the bathroom. I heard a knock at the door.

"Baby, are you okay," Kelvin asked as he leaned over me.

"I don't know, I feel sick," I replied as I got up. I then splashed my face.

"Did you want to try and eat something?" Kelvin asked as he stood on the other side of the bathroom.

"Sure," I replied as we went down stairs into the kitchen. Kelvin then turned on the stove and cracked a few eggs and started cooking them. I felt sick again that smell was overwhelming.

"That smell is gross!" I shouted as I darted for the bathroom

I finally came out and I sat down. The smell of the eggs was making me sick I could barely stand it.

"What has gotten into you?" Kelvin asked as he buttered some toast.

"I don't know but I can't anything," I replied as I rested my head on the table.

"You should try," Kelvin stated.

"I can't I don't know what is wrong with me," I replied.

"Let's go to the doctor," Kelvin replied

"I think I am pregnant." I said looking up at Kelvin.

"That's fast we only made love last night?" Kelvin looked shocked

"Remember, Kelvin, we're not talking about two humans hitching up, things work different in our world." I got ready to go get a pregnancy test.

"True, well I will come with you." Kelvin replied.

We headed for the drug store but the cramping and nausea were unreal I picked up what I wanted and as soon as we got home I dashed to the washroom to do the test. I was so scared I didn't know how to be a parent. I waited 30 seconds and slowly opened my eyes. Sure enough, the device said pregnant. Many things were going through my head like will Kelvin still want me and if not what am I going to do? I won't tell him yet, I thought to myself as I walked out of the washroom.

"Well, honey, are you?" Kelvin asked.

I couldn't lie looking at his cute smile, God he gave me butterflies. I handed him the test device and he stared at it, unsure about what he was seeing.

"Kelvin, dear, it has a positive sign on it. Look"

"You are really pregnant?" Kelvin stared at the test.

"According to this, I am." I said.

"I am happy, but Liz we don't know each other very well. Are you willing to spend forever with me?" Kelvin asked with a worried look on his face.

"Yes, and we will get to know each other, I am sure." I replied reaching up and kissing his lips.

"I guess I am going to be a dad," Kelvin replied.

I needed to find my brother and my father but I had no idea how to get there.

"I am worried about our babies future, you already have to fight for your life if word gets out that you are pregnant do you know what that means?" Kelvin asked as he touched my face and brought me closer to him.

"I know I need to find my family." I said as I took a deep breath in. I didn't know what to think or how to react.

"No Liz you can't trust them." Kelvin said with a stern voice.

"I can't trust my own family?" I said as I looked at him strangely

"It is hard to trust anyone," Kelvin replied.

"They are my family," I stated.

"I realize that but it's for your safety," Kelvin replied.

"I need to though, you don't understand," I said.

"I don't know if it's a good idea," he says as he grabs me.

"Let her go," A voice demanded.

"Hunter," We both said in shock.

"I wasn't going to hurt her I didn't want her to make any wrong decisions." Kelvin let me go.

I hugged Hunter I was so happy to see him.

"Let's go downstairs and have a good conservation," Hunter said as we both followed him to the living room.

I couldn't believe my eyes, I saw my father, Damien, Mark, Jeff, and Blair sitting on the couch. And of course Conrad and the other guards were there as well.

"Liz, dear, are we ever glad we found you," Mark took my hand and sat me down beside him.

"Kelvin it has been a long time," Blair said "Now what is your business with my daughter?" Blair asked.

"Umm, well sir I want to be with her." Kelvin replied.

"Don't we all and what makes you so special to have her?" Damien snapped as he stood up.

"We have a lot in common and we have fun around each other," Kelvin replied.

All the vampires started to fight amongst each other, I got fed up and I stood up and yelled. "Would you all shut the fuck up, I am pregnant," everyone stopped what they were doing and looked at me in complete silence.

"What did you say?" Hunter asked and glared at Kelvin.

"I said I am pregnant." I said in a lower voice.

"How the hell did you get her pregnant?" Damien asked as he crossed his arms.

"Damien because I wasn't ready to have a baby when I was with you, I need to be ready and happy." I replied.

"You weren't happy with me?" Damien asked.

"It wasn't that but I was forced to be with you." I replied.

Mark broke the silence in the room. "Well, now we have to protect you even more," Mark reached over to feel my stomach.

"Liz, are you crazy?" my dad asked.

"I didn't mean to dad, it happened, that's all." I looked away in shame.

I got up and went running upstairs, I was really confused and didn't want to be alone in this.

"Kelvin, so I take it you're the father?" asked Hunter

"Yea I am, and you sound concerned. She is your sister I would never hurt her." "I want her to be with someone who will treat her well," Hunter said.

"I will treat her well." Kelvin said as he got up and went to check up on me.

"Do you trust him, Blair?" Jeff asked.

"I don't know who I can trust," Blair answered.

"Liz, are you okay?" Kelvin asked as he came into the room.

"I don't know. Does my family hate me?" I asked as I stared at the floor.

"No of course they don't, they fear for you that's all." Kelvin hugged me.

"I feel embarrassed and ashamed of myself," I replied as I pulled away from him.

"Don't be things are meant to happen. Now let's go back downstairs," Kelvin said as he held my hand and led me back downstairs.

"Liz, what is wrong?" Jeff asked.

"I don't know, I feel like you guys are disgusted with me and that you hate me." I replied.

"We don't hate you, we are scared for you, Liz, You don't understand that you are the first female hybrid and now you are pregnant," Jeff explained

"What is going to happen to me?" I asked.

"Liz, nothing we are here for you," Mark butted in.

"But I always seem to be getting kidnapped and attacked." I replied. I need some time to myself please," I said as I got up and got my shoes on. I started walking and I found a park nearby so I decided to relax on a swing.

"I will go find her and make sure is alright, she shouldn't be alone," Hunter replied as he sighed and stood up. He got on his shoes and headed outside. It didn't take him long to find me sitting on a swing.

"Liz you can't always run away it is too dangerous outside for you," Hunter explained to me.

"I know I need some time to think." I replied.

"I understand you have a lot to deal with," Hunter replied.

"Hunter, do you think it's wrong that I got pregnant?" I asked looking up at him.

"It's your choice," Hunter replied. "Come on, Liz, let's go back." Hunter said.

We made it back home, but something felt wrong. I had a horrible feeling.

"Liz, Hunter get out now!" Mark yelled as he started screaming.

"I don't think so," A voice yelled as he blocked the door. I turned around and there was a mean looking vampire standing there. Her long black hair covered her face she was wearing a black leather suit she stood there grinning at me.

"Alexandra, come do something with this male vampire," the master vampire commanded Alexandra.

"Yes sir," Alexandra replied as she went to Hunter and zapped him. I couldn't move.

"So sweetheart what is your name?" A shorter stalky vampire asked me as he tied his brown hair up and scratched his face with his sharp nails his brown eyes stared down at me.

"L…L…Liz," I answered.

"Well Liz my name is Tony I am the strongest and oldest vampire, I was called out by a friend of mine. Does the name Caleb sound familiar?" Tony asked as he checked me out.

"I had my run in with Caleb." I replied.

"He told me all about you and I had to find you for myself?" Tony asked as he grabbed me and threw onto the couch.

"Please don't hurt my family," I blurted out.

"I won't hurt them much if you cooperate, dear," Tony answered as he back handed Mark.

"Okay I will. Please, no more," I started sobbing.

Tony back handed me, picked me and chucked me across the room.

"Please don't, I am pregnant," I got up as I started to cry.

"Really, now you are an interesting girl," Tony walked over to me.

"What do you want?" I asked.

"Well I was going to take you and call you mine, but now that I found you I want to show you something first," Tony grabbed my arm and dragged me outside and tossed me his van. His other vampire guards had my family in a different vehicle I had to drive with Tony alone.

"Did you know I was a hybrid?" I asked him.

"Yeah, female hybrids have such a sweet smell to them," Tony replied as he stared at me.

"Are you going to hurt me and my family?" I asked.

"It depends if you guys are good and listen to me," Tony put his hand on my leg.

We arrived at a broken down warehouse, the windows were all smashed out and the air smelt disgusting. We walked inside and I couldn't believe my eyes. Tyler and Steven were tied to a chair.

Chapter Eleven

THE ULTIMATE CHOICE

"Tyler, Steven what is going on?" I asked as I ran to them.

"My dear, they are disgusting werewolves and I want you to kill them, if you can do that I will never bother you and your family again," Tony explained as hovered around me.

"No I can't and I won't," I hissed as I shoved Tony out of the way.

"You're a pathetic bitch you care about these wolves more than your own family?" Tony replied as he grabbed Hunter and took out a stake.

"No, please don't, I will do anything. Please don't hurt him," I begged.

"Okay, well then honey, kill these wolves," Tony demanded as he went over towards them.

"Liz, no don't I am sorry I hurt you," Tyler begged me.

I was trying to think of a plan to get all of us out but there were too many vampires, then I thought about something I saw in a movie with werewolves. I started howling and Tyler and Steven clued in they to began howling.

"What the fuck are you doing little girl?" Tony hissed as he grabbed me and threw me onto the floor.

I started laughing, I could smell other wolves surrounding the building it was a matter of time before they all came barging in.

"Why are you laughing? What is going on?" Tony screamed as he grabbed a stake and flipped me over onto my back. "Tell me what is happening or I will end your life right here." Tony snarled and held me down.

"You will see in about 2 seconds." I dug my nails deep into his face and pushed him off. By the time I got up and there were about 20 wolves crashing through the door growling and showing their teeth, their hackles were standing straight up.

"You bitch, so this was your master plan to call other wolves to help you!" Tony reached for a gun.

I growled and gave the signal to the wolves to start their attack. They went straight for Tony. In the meantime I untied Steven and Tyler. We managed to get out of there as fast as we could.

"Liz, thank you," Tyler said smiling.

"You're welcome." I replied.

"We should get out of here," Hunter said as we jumped into a truck and took off. We could hear screams and gun shots coming from the shack.

"Liz, I am sorry about what I said the last time we were together," Tyler apologized.

"It is alright, but I am with someone else and I am pregnant now," I explained to him.

"What, a vampire?" Tyler asked as he looked angry.

"Yes," I answered and turned to face Kelvin.

We made it back home safe and sound. I felt nervous with Tyler and Steven being around as we jumped out of the truck and piled into the house. I was so exhausted I sat down on the couch and fell asleep.

"Is Liz sleeping?" Steven asked Tyler.

"Yeah, she is, leave her," Hunter replied as he handed Tyler and Steven a glass of water.

"Who is the father of her baby?" Tyler asked in disgust.

"I am," Kelvin replied as he sat down on a chair.

"I can't believe I made the stupid choice of not wanting to be with her," Tyler said as he knelt down beside me.

"I can't believe you let her go either." Steven went into the kitchen.

"You're not helping, Steven," Tyler hissed as he got up and followed Steven into the kitchen.

"You two cut it out, what is done is done," Hunter said as he put a blanket over me.

It was getting late and everyone crashed. I woke up around 4 am and went to the kitchen to grab a drink.

"Hey, baby," Kelvin whispered in my ear as he put his hands on my hips and kissed my neck.

"You scared me, honey," I replied and around to kiss him. He lifted me up onto the counter and started kissing me. He took my shirt off and pulled his pants down a bit and we made love. It felt so good to get some stress released. Kelvin and I fell asleep upstairs on one of the beds we both woke up to banging and water being poured.

"What's all the ruckus?" I asked as I got closer to the noise.

I saw a lady rummaging through some stuff she was throwing everything onto the floor and breaking things.

"Excuse me, who the hell are you and what are you doing?" I asked as I stepped closer towards her.

"You scared me, my name is Natasha and I am a friend of Kelvin's," Natasha answered as she stared at me with her green eyes then turn her back to me and continued rummaging through everything. Her short dirty blonde hair was done up in a bun she was wearing a purple head band her clothing seemed too small they clung on to her small petite frame.

I went upstairs to find Kelvin I wanted to see what the hell she was doing here.

"Kelvin, are you awake?" I asked as I pounced on him.

"Now I am," he replied.

"Your friend Natasha is here and she is rummaging through everything downstairs."

"What?" Kelvin looked surprised and went running downstairs. He pinned Natasha against the wall and started yelling at her.

"It is nice to see you to, Kelvin," Natasha replied as she shoved him away.

"What are you doing here? I made it very clear that I didn't want to see you the last time we were together," Kelvin snapped at Natasha.

"Why, I missed you baby," Natasha replied as she tried to kiss him.

"Don't touch me, you disgust me," Kelvin snapped and shoved her away.

"Why? Do you have another lover?" Natasha glared at me as I came down the stairs.

"Actually, yeah, he does, bitch, me," I hissed as I went and kissed Kelvin.

"You're dating the wolf bitch?" Natasha asked as she looked surprised.

"Yeah and she is a hybrid, plus she is pregnant with my kid," Kelvin kissed me.

"What? You got her pregnant?" Natasha stormed into the living room and started crying.

"Natasha I know you probably hate me, but what is wrong?" I sat beside her.

"I don't hate you, I am jealous of you, I loved Kelvin," Natasha cried.

"You will find someone, you are pretty." I hugged her.

"Are you really pregnant with his child?" Natasha looked at my stomach.

"Yeah I am." I replied.

"Liz, leave her, let's go for a walk," Kelvin demanded as he headed for the front door.

"Okay," I replied and followed him outside.

"Liz, I didn't want you to meet her, she is nothing but trouble. I dated her a while back and she grew very possessive and I don't know if she will do anything to you now that she knows that you are mine." Kelvin put his arm around me.

"How did she find you," I asked.

"She had a witch put a spell on me so she can track me, I told you possessive," Kelvin answered.

"Yeah, she seems like the possessive type, I was trying to be a friend maybe calm her down before things got ugly," I explained.

"You don't want to be nice to her, she will use you." Kelvin drew me closer and held me.

"I am sick of fighting, I want this all to end," I mumbled into his chest as he hugged me.

"I know, honey, but for now we have to watch our backs," Kelvin turned back towards home.

We made it back home when I dropped to the floor in unexplainable pain. It felt like someone was stabbing me in my stomach over and over again.

"Someone hurry help me," Kelvin screamed as he lay me on my side.

"What is going on? She is bleeding!" Hunter picked me up and put me in his vehicle.

"Where are you taking her?" Kelvin asked.

"To the hospital Kelvin she is pregnant, remember," Hunter sped off.

They got me out of the vehicle and into the hospital as I was rushed into the emergency room.

"Doctor, help her please, she is pregnant," Kelvin begged as he started to cry.

"Okay, calm down. What is her name?" asked the doctor as he took my blood pressure.

"Her name is Liz, and she is my girlfriend." Kelvin stated.

"Okay, I will do some tests if you would please go and wait in the waiting room." The doctor insisted.

When I woke up they were doing an ultrasound and taking a blood sample.

"Doctor, come look at this," said the nurse he came and took a look at the ultrasound.

"It looks like this baby is growing at a rapid speed, according to this sheet her boyfriend said she found out she was pregnant only a couple weeks ago. But according to this ultrasound it looks like she is already 3 months pregnant." The nurse shot the doctor a confused look.

"What's happening to me?" I asked as I coughed a few times and tried to focus on my surroundings everything was too blurry I couldn't make out anything.

"Well, Liz, you are at the hospital. My name is Dr. Fritz, your boyfriend was worried that whatever was going on had something to do with your baby." Dr. Fritz took a cold cloth and wiped my forehead with it.

"I remember falling to the floor in a lot of pain and there was blood. Is my baby okay?" I asked preparing myself for the worse.

"Yes, your baby is fine, but your boyfriend said you found out you were pregnant about two weeks ago. Well according to this ultrasound you appear to be about three months pregnant." Dr. Fritz furrowed his brow.

"Maybe I didn't have symptoms until now," I replied, nervous that he might find out that I am half werewolf and half vampire and that my boyfriend is also a vampire.

"That could be possible, but we are going to have to keep you here until we can figure what out what is really going on. Dr. Fritz poured me a glass of water all I could think about was blood. I could hear his heart pumping with blood but I had to control myself.

Shortly after the doctor and the nurse left, Kelvin and Hunter walked in.

"How are you feeling?" Kelvin asked.

"I feel weak," I replied as I tried sitting up.

"Don't move, just rest," Hunter said.

I nodded and closed my eyes then I was out cold. I woke up a few hours later and Hunter and Kelvin were nowhere to be seen. I tried to fall asleep again but I was so hungry. I lay there thinking and wondering if I could finally live my life with my family. Ever since I became a hybrid I had this fantasy that I would be with my family and we might live a decent life together, not having to worry. But that isn't the case and I am always running in fear, always fighting. I was almost asleep again when I heard screams coming from down the hall. I wanted to go check it out but I was still too weak. I opened my eyes and looked around and saw a dark figure in the corner of room.

"Who is there?" I said as I tried pushing the button for a nurse.

"Ah, I see that you are awake. How lovely, now I can get down to business," the voice answered as he came closer to me.

"Who are you?" I asked as I tried to focus on him.

"That is not important, but what is important is that you cooperate with me," the man touched my stomach and I froze in fear.

"What do you want?" I asked.

"I saw those other vampires leave your room so that makes me believe that you are a vampire to so that must mean that you believe in werewolves too, so my question is do you know where I can find our hybrid?" He knelt down beside me.

"I d..don't know," I replied hoping he would go away.

"Now sweetheart I know that you are lying to me, I can tell by the way you answered me. I don't want to hurt you, but I will if you leave me with no choice." The man touched my face.

"The hybrid is my best friend. Her name is Stacey and she lives in Ontario," I replied hoping he would believe me.

"See honey that wasn't so hard now. What does she look like?" The man replied.

"She is tiny, brown short hair, brown eyes and has a moon tattoo on her wrist," I lied.

"Thank you, that is all I needed to know," and he took out his phone.

"What are your plans with the hybrid?" I asked not really wanting to know.

"That is none of your concern," The man replied as he left the room.

I could hear him talking with someone outside.

"Hey Kevin, yeah I am going to go to Ontario and find our hybrid," The man said to Kevin.

"Brett, how did you know where the hybrid was?" Kevin asked.

"The girl in that room told me, I saw her with two other vampires," Brett explained.

"What does that girl look like?" Kevin asked.

"I didn't get a good look, why?" Brett asked as they turned on the light and walked into my room. By then I got out of bed and hid from them. "Where the fuck did she go?" Brett hissed as he threw the blankets all over the floor.

"That girl that usually hangs out with vampires her name is Liz and she is the hybrid," Kevin explained.

I was shaking, I was so weak and scared and I needed to escape. I kept looking to see if they were around and there was no sign of them. I got up slowly and ran for the door, as soon as I turned the corner I ran right into Kevin.

"Hello baby, remember me?" Kevin asked as he laughed and held on to me.

"Let me go, you sick fuck." I kicked and punched him.

"Well, well, well so you think you can lie to me and get away with it?" Brett snapped as he back handed me.

I had a good look at the man that was in my room. His tall frame hovered over me, when he hit me it felt like I was hit with a hammer his brown eyes glared down at me his brown hair was spiked I could smell the gel he had put in his hair.

"I almost succeeded," I said laughing in his face.

"You sure are a pretty girl and vey feisty, I must say," Brett licked my face.

"Get away!" I kicked him and elbowed Kevin.

"You bitch," Kevin groaned and he let me go. I took off running but they were right behind me.

"You can't run forever," Brett yelled.

I felt so weak I couldn't run anymore, I stopped and then collapsed.

"Now we have the bitch and this time there is no escape," Kevin said as he picked me up. I woke up a few hours later in a dark room, I didn't remember what happened. I got up and looked around the room, it was dark except for a little light that came through a small keyhole on the door. I went over there to peak through it and saw a man outside the door.

"Hello excuse me, but where am I?" I asked.

"You are a prisoner of Brett's," the guard answered me.

I slid down the wall and started to cry. I soon heard footsteps coming towards my room and then door opened and a man appeared in the light.

"Get up baby cakes I need answers," Brett demanded and grabbed me and lifted me up.

"First things first are you going to lie to me again?" Brett asked as he smelled my hair.

"No," I answered as I backed away.

"Good, so you are the hybrid then how come you were in the hospital?" Brett asked as he held onto my arm.

"I am pregnant and I was in a lot of pain," I answered as I tried to break free.

"You're pregnant? That is interesting," Brett seemed surprised.

He dragged me upstairs to where a lot of vampires and humans were. Brett shoved me towards Kevin.

"Well, Liz, now that we finally have you, what should we do with you?" Kevin asked, slowly..

"Let me go," I said. Like that was going to happen. "Someone will come for me, you watch," and I glared at him.

"Like who? No-one knows that you are here," Kevin said as he grabbed me and threw me into a different room. I needed to escape I was so weak and hungry and there was no way I could fight. Suddenly, the door opened and Brett came inside the room he then injected something into my neck everything went fuzzy and I collapsed.

"Pick her up and put her on that bed," Brett demanded Kevin as he picked Liz up and strapped her to a bed.

I woke up a few times and everything was still fuzzy I wasn't awake for very long.

"I wonder how long until she gives birth?" Kevin asked.

"I don't know I am not a doctor. We will keep her here as long as it takes though," Brett replied.

Meanwhile back at the hospital Hunter and Kelvin come back to see me.

"Hunter she is gone!" Kelvin shouted he started looking everywhere and throwing things around.

"What. Wait I smell other vampires I bet someone found out she was here," Hunter replied.

"Yeah your right," A women replied as she stood at the door way. She stared at the vampires with her blue eyes her grey hair was braided back she wore a purple crystal around her neck.

"Who are you?" Hunter asked as he went darting at her.

The women stuck her hand out and Hunter collapsed to the floor holding his head.

"You're a witch," Kelvin said surprisingly.

"Yes I am I am also Liz's mother Jane," Jane replied as she walked towards Hunter.

Hunter stood up still holding his head. "Was that necessary?" Hunter asked.

"Not really. We are wasting time boys lets go find Liz," Jane demanded. "Anyways you boys go home I will get Liz," Jane explained.

"How do you know where she is?" Kelvin asked.

"It won't be hard to find out," Jane replied.

Meanwhile I started to open my eyes I looked around a bit the pain was over baring.

I forced myself to sit up in this uncomfortable bed. I turned my body and let my legs hang over the bed for a few seconds until I caught my breath. I sighed and dropped down on to the floor. I slowly made it to the door I swung the door open and there stood Kevin he smiled at me.

"Hello darling. I see you awake and ready for the day," Kevin said as he came closer to me.

"What did you do to me? Why are you doing this?" I asked as I backed up.

"Oh honey so many questions you will find out soon enough," Kevin replied as he went behind me and shoved me out into the hall way.

"Hello, Liz. I see you are awake. Now let us get on with business, shall we?" Brett said as he gave me an evil smirk.

"What did you do to me?" I asked.

"We just gave you something to do knock you out," Brett replied.

Before there was more said there was a knock at the door.

"Go get that," Brett ordered Kevin.

Jane was standing there.

"Who are you? What do you want?" Kevin growled.

"My name is Jane and I am here to see Liz," Jane answered.

"How do you know Liz?" Kevin asked.

"That is none of your concern," Jane answered as she shoved Kevin out of the way.

Jane knew exactly where I was. And she found me. We just stopped and stared at each other.

Chapter Twelve

THE LAST PIECE OF THE PUZZLE

"Liz, is that you dear?" Jane asked as she started to cry.

"Yes, and who are you?" I asked.

"My name is Jane and, Liz, I am you're mother" Jane replied.

"What? My mom passed away when I was a child," I replied.

"No honey. That is what I wanted them to tell you. I wanted you to live a somewhat normal life. I knew that you would find out sooner or later. I am sorry this had to happen to you," Jane explained to me as she put her arms around me. Brett was behind her and he started clapping.

"Great, now that we have the mother and daughter both here, let's get this party started!" Brett said laughing.

"I don't think so. You are going to let us both leave," Jane snarled as she started chanting some words it sounded like Spanish. The whole room started to shake pictures where falling off the walls, the windows were smashing. Kelvin and Brett fell to the floor covering their ears.

"Hurry, honey, let's go I will explain everything." Jane held onto me and we took off running. We made it back to my place as we walked in and Hunter, my dad, Mark, Jeff, Trevor, and Damien where sitting in the living room.

"Hey guys!" I said to the boys as they looked at me in excitement.

"Liz, you are alright," Everyone said and came and hugged me.

"Yeah I guess I am alright," I answered back.

"What happened?" Mark asked.

"I was kidnapped by a vampire Brett and his accomplice Kevin. They took me back to their place and I was knocked out," I explained.

"Who is that lady with you?" Jeff asked.

"Her name is Jane, she is my mother." I said.

"Jane, is that really you?" Blair asked.

"Blair?" Jane asked as she hesitated for a bit.

"Yes," Blair answered with a smile.

"Thank you for saving Liz," Blair said.

"It was my pleasure I figure I should help out sometime," Jane replied.

"What did they want with her any ideas?" Hunter asked.

"I am assuming it has something to do with her baby and that diamond," Jane explained.

"I think they were planning on keeping me there until my baby was born. And what exactly is with this diamond?" I asked.

"That diamond is very powerful it will let vampires walk in the day and they will have no weaknesses," Jane explained.

"How come these vampires can walk in the day?" I asked.

"They have a witches spell casted on them already," Jane replied.

"Not to worry anyone but when am I supposed to be having this baby, because I am cramping really bad?" I asked I looked down I saw blood. "I am bleeding what is happening?" I asked as I started to shake.

"You're a hybrid honey you should be due right away. Hybrids pregnancy cycle is much faster and shorter than a human's cycle," Jane explained.

"Ok that is fantastic what do I do know?" I asked.

"I will need lots of towels and a pail of warm water," Jane replied.

"Ok I will grab that stuff," Kelvin said as he went into the kitchen and grabbed a pail of warm water and went to the linen closet and grabbed four big black towels.

"Ok honey lie down and breathe for me ok," Jane said as she helped me lie on the floor.

"It hurts!" I shouted as I breathed fast.

"I know honey take deep breathes in. I can see the baby's head you're doing great honey," Jane replied as I felt the baby come out. A few seconds later I could hear crying.

"You had a girl Liz," Jane said smiling. "Can someone grab me scissors though?" Jane asked as she stared at the baby and rocked her back in forth.

"Here you go," Hunter said handing Jane a pair of scissors.

Jane then cut the umbilical cord. Kelvin then came around and helped me sit up then Jane passed me my baby.

"She is so cute what should we name her?" I asked Kelvin as I kissed my baby.

"How about we name her Celina?" Kelvin suggested as he rubbed my back.

"That is a cute name," I said smiling staring into her eyes she had the biggest blue eyes ever and short fine blonde hair.

I then handed Celina over to Kelvin. "I am going to clean up, mom can you come with me?" I asked as I headed up the stairs.

"Sure honey," Jane replied following me she was hanging on to me making sure I didn't fall.

"She is so cute I can't believe she is mine," Kelvin replied as he walked back and forth with Celina in his arms.

"I know she is adorable. I am worried that those other two will stop at nothing to steal Celina," Blair replied.

"I know I think we are all scared for that," Hunter said.

Meanwhile I am getting ready to have a shower I turn the taps on and mom help me climb into the tub.

"Mom do you think I will ever be safe?" I asked as I stood under the warm water.

"I don't know honey. I can't answer that for you but you will always have your family to protect you," Jane replied.

"Thanks. I am worried for Celina," I replied as I finished washing up I turned off the taps and stuck my head out of the shower curtains.

"That is the consequences of bringing a hybrid child into the world my dear," Jane answered as she handed me a towel.

"I know I just don't know how to protect her," I said drying off and slipping into a night gown.

"Maybe you will have to give her out for adoption like Blair and I did," Jane said as she gave me a serious look.

"I can't," I replied as I went into my bed room. I noticed a crib and some toys in the corner. "Mom, where did this stuff come from?" I asked smiling.

"Kelvin and Hunter went shopping," Jane replied as she rubbed my back.

"Do you like this stuff?" Kelvin asked as he walked towards the crib and placed Celina inside.

"Yes do I ever," I said my voice was full of excitement.

"Enjoy honey I am going to go get ready for bed see you two love birds in the morning," Jane said as she blew me a kiss.

"Good night mother," I replied blowing her a kiss back.

Kelvin and I got ready for bed. Kelvin cuddled right up to me he put his arm around me and kissed my cheek.

"Good night my love," Kelvin said.

"Good night baby," I replied.

I woke up to a loud thump coming from downstairs. I got up and went downstairs to investigate. I saw nothing but one of the windows in the living room wide open the curtains were flapping as the cool breeze came through the window. I went over and shut it then I felt something run past me I quickly turned and there was nothing. I then head Kelvin freaking out upstairs I ran upstairs.

"What is it?" I asked panicking.

"Celina, she is gone!" Kelvin shouted.

"What how?" I asked as I went running back downstairs.

"What is going on?" Hunter asked as he slowly came downstairs rubbing his eyes and yawning.

"Celina is gone," I replied I broke down in tears.

Moments after the phone rang. I walked towards the phone and picked it up.

"Hello," I answered.

"Hello Liz, if you ever want to see your baby again you will have to meet us by the river bank by your place at 5:00 am sharp this morning and you must come alone," The man replied. His voice sounded familiar it was very deep.

"I will do whatever just don't hurt my baby," I said sobbing. I looked over at the clock it read 4:00 am I was filled with anxiety.

"Good girl," The man replied as he hung up.

I hung up and dropped the phone on to the floor and went and sat down on the couch. I just sat there in silence.

"Liz what is it who was that?" Blair asked.

"I don't know who but they have Celina and they want me to meet them at the river bank nearby in an hour and no one can come," I replied as I paced back and forth the living room.

"I will cast a spell on you honey so they can't hurt you," Jane said.

"Yeah we will have to think something," I said as I kept staring at the clock it seemed like the clock was getting louder and louder.

"We will honey we are here for you," Jane said as she got out her brown witch book.

Time was ticking and I was getting very anxious I had no idea what to expect or even worse am I going to get out of this alive?

CPSIA information can be obtained at www.ICGtesting.com
Printed in the USA
LVOW08s0619300414

383746LV00001B/4/P